BAILIE'S WAKE

LP HIL
Hill, Pamela
Bailie's wake

DATE DUE

Willimantic Library Service Cen[illegible]
1320 Main St., Suite 25
Willimantic, CT 06226

DEMCO

BAILIE'S WAKE

Pamela Hill

Willimantic Library Service Center
1320 Main St., Suite 25
Willimantic, CT 06226

Chivers Press
Bath, England

G.K. Hall & Co.
Thorndike, Maine USA

This Large Print edition is published by Chivers Press, England, and by G.K. Hall & Co., USA.

Published in 2000 in the U.K. by arrangement with Robert Hale, Ltd.

Published in 2000 in the U.S. by arrangement with Robert Hale, Ltd.

U.K. Hardcover ISBN 0-7540-4210-3 (Chivers Large Print)
U.K. Softcover ISBN 0-7540-4211-1 (Camden Large Print)
U.S. Softcover ISBN 0-7838-9100-8 (Nightingale Series Edition)

Copyright © Pamela Hill 2000

The right of Pamela Hill to be identified as the author of this work has been asserted by her in accordance with the Copyright, Designs and Patents Act 1988.

All rights reserved.

The text of this Large Print edition is unabridged.
Other aspects of the book may vary from the original edition.

Set in 16 pt. New Times Roman.

Printed in Great Britain on acid-free paper.

British Library Cataloguing in Publication Data available

Library of Congress Cataloging-in-Publication Data

Hill, Pamela.
Bailie's wake / Pamela Hill.
p. cm.
ISBN 0-7838-9100-8 (lg. print : sc : alk. paper)
1. Glasgow (Scotland)—Fiction. 2. Large type books. I. Title.
PR6058.I446 B35 2000
823'.914—dc21 00–039596

AUTHOR'S NOTE

The episode about the pillow is true and took place in genteel Glasgow in the 1850s. My grandmother heard it whispered, in strict confidence, during her girlhood there in the 1860s. I mention the matter in case anyone thinks it could not have happened even then.

P.H.

PART I

CHAPTER ONE

Several persons were listening to the new minister's hellfire sermon, including himself. That was at the beginning; by the end, although the Reverend Aeneas McPhail remained aware of the sonorous echoes of his own deep voice proclaiming the likelihood of what would happen on the Day of Judgment, his attention had been caught, at least for the time, by worldly things.

It was some months now since he had sustained the charge, as they called it, of Oakdale parish, Glasgow. He had succeeded old Dr Swords, who had died unexpectedly, leaving a widow who had never said much and who was still here. As for Oakdale itself, it was prosperous, the congregation being made up mostly of the merchant classes, which meant money and respectability. As regarded the rest, as the chief subscriber to the newly erected parish church itself, Sir Phelim Orde—he was of course present today—had jocularly remarked, there weren't any oaks or any dale, but they had to call it something. As Sir Phelim's elegant rebuilding of red sandstone flats in the area had led to a need for new parish boundaries in the first place, nobody answered back.

Sir Phelim sat now, with his young second

wife, in the notable front side pew. They had come up by river in Sir Phelim's private paddle-steamer and from there, by waiting carriage as usual. During the week Sir Phelim maintained a small coach-house not far from the manse itself, but it was still a considerable journey to make from his Clydeside mansion each Sunday. No doubt he felt he owed it to his position.

This put the minister in a slight quandary. He knew he must turn, now and again, his own majestic black-haired head—his side-whiskers were said to be the finest in Glasgow—and the glare of his fierce dark Highland eyes in that direction, at least enough to make Sir Phelim feel he was getting his money's worth. One had of course to do the same for most of the well-found congregation, seated here in their variously rented pews and rustling, at least as far as the ladies were concerned, with bright plain aniline-dyed silks and French velvets and, at this season, sealskin fur. A faint aroma of moth-balls, perspiration and false teeth rose to the pulpit, inevitably wafted there by the collective warmth of Oakdale's regular attendance.

The trouble with looking, as duty required, at Sir Phelim's pew meant that one could not help looking at the same time at his wife. It was enough to give the sermon pause; Lady Orde today was wearing yet another bonnet that matched her pelisse, and a wine-coloured velvet gown. Her little hands were in a muff. The minister had already taken all of it in, and was reproachfully aware that he could not have told what his own wife had on except that it was as usual, seated doucely as she was beside her mother and old Mrs Swords in the manse pew at the back. However, Amy never dressed in a way that would be noticed by anyone. She was a subdued creature, as was no doubt proper. Lady Orde—the simile occurred to him in the midst of the delivery about hellfire—was like a bright flower among cabbages. She must be a good thirty years younger than her husband: maybe more.

At the foot of the pulpit steps sat the beadle in all his glory, and not far off the session clerk, Joseph Sproat, waited to take the collection. This was his moment of weekly importance, to be seen by all with the large brass plate, rapidly filling up with sovereigns and silver coins as he passed it round. Sproat himself was a small man, and the occasion itself made him feel larger. In feature he could be uncharitably described as ratlike, except for neatly trimmed fair side-whiskers, and a certain air of prudent persuasion useful in insurance. His impeccable lum hat—they had grown taller this year—lay beside him where he presently sat, upturned to show its white silk lining, with the name of an expensive hatter displayed on the label. Mr Sproat was doing well in his insurance business, also in the cotton-mill he owned, situated to the north of the city. He was always careful to move in the right mercantile circles and to achieve the right depth of civic bow. He was already a councillor, and had a coldly fixed ambition to become a bailie. He was unmarried.

He stared between lowered eyelids at the inhabitants of the manse pew. It was always as well to keep in with the minister, while at the same time not altogether permitting him to forget his place. The small grey-green eyes passed by young Mrs McPhail, who did not interest Sproat—they said she had expectations from an uncle, however—and her grenadier of a mother, likewise the widow of the late Dr Swords, who still sat there in her black weepers although everyone said she should have moved out by now instead of staying on meantime in a floor of the Bath Street manse itself. Having flicked a pale and assessing glance over all these, Sproat let his gaze dwell for instants on Nancy Purdie, the between-maid from Bath Street, whose situation he had himself obtained for her only lately by way of earlier employment at the mill. Nancy also cleaned the church, by arrangement, on Mondays, it not being permitted to do so on the Sabbath after the second service, which itself meant a further sermon to attend in the late afternoon. There was no doubt that, having had the week virtually free to prepare his two addresses, the minister had to work hard on Sundays. Well, other folk worked during the week; and Nancy, who unlike many young Glasgow working-class women did not have bandy legs but good plump straight ones, would give satisfaction in certain other ways to Mr Sproat when he came down, having deposited the collected sovereigns in the Bank, to inspect everything in time for the ensuing Sabbath. Nancy would convey her comforts thereafter on the vestry bench without fuss for fourpence, at the same time giving Mr Sproat any news worth having from the manse and elsewhere. By now, the arrangement was almost domestic.

Sproat's glance then shifted briefly, for it was not advisable to be seen to stare at young Lady Orde, glorious as the sight was. As he had long ago decided, she was a fine piece, no doubt like a newly ripened peach when undressed, but hardly his for the plucking. One could look from time to time, and imagine, which cost nothing, but it was a mistake for any man to set his sights too high when he had his way to make as things were.

The Reverend McPhail gave his penultimate roar about sheep and goats and the necessity of avoiding the wrath to come, then vanished for some time below the pulpit's rim, ostensibly in prayer. Everyone breathed more freely, reticules were opened and waistcoat pockets delved into, the precentor intoned the next paraphrase tabulated on the board—it had been thought a trifle daring to instal an organ quite yet, though the matter was being considered by the more forward-looking of the elders—and the Oakdale congregation got up, rustling predictably, to sing. Glasgow being a musical city, there were many fine voices, and the result was gratifying. Presently they sat down again, the minister reappeared, and heads were bowed for his long impromptu prayer such as followed all singing.

Amy McPhail bowed her head like the rest, because Mama was sitting next to her as usual and, beyond that, Mrs Swords. Amy did not know which of the two ladies frightened her more, but the worst fear of all, and it happened whenever he was getting ready one of his sermons on the previous night, was the crushing, stifling swiftness and unpredictability of the marital act, in bed with Mr McPhail; it had never occurred to Amy to call him anything else. They had been married now for four years, beginning at Kilbeg, his former charge, where she had lived with Mama till then. Whatever it was that was expected of her as a result of everything hadn't happened, although Mama kept asking; certainly it seemed to help the sermons when the minister behaved as he had last night. Amy herself didn't ask more and never had; some things weren't mentioned or explained. Regarding marriage as a condition of life, all she had been told at the time was that Mr McPhail had proposed, evidently by way of Mama, and that, being already twenty-five, she, Amy, had best accept, as the minister was certainly not a fortune-hunter like some. Amy had been warned all her life against fortune-hunters, as it was expected that there would be some money from Great-uncle Julius, who had served in his time in the Honourable East India Company and had, as Mama mysteriously stated, shaken the pagoda tree to some effect. He lived now in a remote shooting lodge in the Highlands with his guru, whose name was Ahur and who, Mama said again, was fortunately not interested in worldly goods; in fact he wore nothing but a loin-cloth and sat mostly cross-legged in contemplation on the floor. Amy remembered seeing him thus once as a child, then had been hastily taken by the hand and led away. She remembered also, from those days, a little Gaelic; it helped the young manse coachman, who was waiting outside now with the horses. It was never possible for coachmen to come to church, but one thing that had been specially designed at Oakdale was a wide sweep of circular carriageway outside, where they could remain comfortably seated till it was time to drive back. The coachman's name was Seumas, and he had red hair. He had been here since Dr Swords' day, so he must have excellent references. He certainly managed the horses very well.

* * *

Louisa McKitterick, Amy's mother, as usual formidably attired in jet bugles, had not been listening to the sermon; she had heard a good many like it before. It was an opportunity instead to observe other things and to think separate thoughts than those enunciated by her son-in-law, in telling fashion, from the pulpit. Mr McPhail—no more than Amy herself did the minister's mother-in-law call him anything else—had his head full of theology, Greek, Hebrew, history, and Latin, having studied most thoroughly at Glasgow University as a young man. All this Louisa had ascertained before considering him as a husband for her only child and, in the ordinary way, source of great financial prospects by inheritance. However, Uncle Julius's mind did not work in exactly the way it ought, and he had told her, Louisa, his late brother's only daughter, to her face years ago that he wasn't goin' to leave his money to any fool of a woman, and provided Amy married some feller who wasn't a fortune-hunter, and could keep her in decency, the money would go to the first son they had assumin' he wasn't an idiot or a hunchback. Otherwise, Ahur here would be left the lot and would give it away to the poor of Madras.

Louisa had been determined from then on that the poor of Madras should not have it, and so intently had she pursued this ambition that Amy was never allowed to meet any young or irresponsible male or to attend frivolous events. As the poor child had no talents in particular, this meant no life at all. In fact, her mother surrounded Amy McKitterick like a hermit crab's shell from the time Amy could walk, seldom allowed her out of her sight, educated her herself at home in such things as a young girl ought to know and nothing they shouldn't, and in general denied her the development of any identity except that of a wordless slave. However, even a slave, once married, ought to multiply; and therein lay the source of Mrs McKitterick's growing anxiety, as after four years, and certain undoubted sounds made with frequency by Mr McPhail through the adjoining bedroom wall at Kilbeg and, later, Bath Street, there was still no sign of a pending happy event, and Uncle Julius by now was seventy-four.

Louisa thought of him briefly and without affection. He had been married long ago in India, the marriage had not been a success, and the wife had, one understood, returned to her family, leaving one son on whom Uncle Julius had doted. Young Nicholas, her cousin, had been reared like a prince, procured a commission later in a famous regiment, and had promptly been killed at Sebastopol amid the brave unforgotten skirl of the Ladies from Hell, the 42nd. It was thought that Uncle Julius attached himself closely to the guru because Ahur could in some way keep him in touch with the dead boy's ghost; but that was none of Louisa's business. She herself, or at least Amy, should in nature have been named as heirs. It remained to do something about the existing situation; it seemed probable, by now, that Amy was perhaps not capable of bearing children. That the whole thing could be Mr McPhail's fault was most unlikely; one had only to look at him, or failing that to listen.

While the rich deep voice of her son-in-law thundered on from the pulpit's height at the far end of the church, Mrs McKitterick's small and observant hazel eye went on taking in details from beneath her bugled bonnet. To the left, the widow Swords was meantime completely obscured by the black crape weepers she insisted on maintaining, and anyway one saw too much of her all of every day; it was time she went, she had plenty of money from a previous marriage and could go where she liked. Louisa's eyes therefore slewed round, past the sight of that dreadful session-clerk Sproat—Sir Phelim, in a moment's jocularity, had, one understood, referred to him as Holy Joe, but one must on no account spread *that*—past Sir Phelim and his opulent and brazen young wife, who had deliberately loosened her pelisse to show off the curves of an alluring velvet-covered bosom, contriving to make the whole thing look accidental. However, Louisa knew about her already from Mrs McIntyre, the celebrated headmistress, who sat now further back with the selected few of her young ladies who could afford the extra charge, or their parents could, of a shared carriage to Oakdale. Brabazon Orde had once been one of them, from nowhere in particular. Sir Phelim was, of course, a governor, and having seen Brabazon once finished, proposed immediately. There it was, and as the young woman had no money of her own the marriage had been most fortunate for her.

* * *

In the end, just before the sermon wound to some predictable conclusion, the merciless gaze returned, past poor Amy, to Louisa's own manse pew, where at the end, in suitably humble garb and with clean hands, sat Nancy Purdie, the between-maid with the additional task, in here, of Monday cleaning. That aspect interested Mrs McKitterick less for the moment, although she took an informed interest as a rule, than Nancy's physical appearance, particularly her dark hair and eyes. She was a sonsie creature, high-coloured, with a full bosom and buttocks on which she at present quite naturally sat, but one had noticed their plump contours occasionally while the young woman blacked the manse grates. Purdie was a good worker. There was no doubt, also, that in the event—and the event was beginning to take forbidden but urgent shape in Louisa McKitterick's totally conscienceless upper mind—she would prove fertile. If mated to a man with dark eyes and hair like her own, she would almost certainly produce a child of that colouring, to be described, perhaps, to Uncle Julius as closely resembling its father.

The daring of her own thoughts—they must have been stirring for some time—gave even Louisa pause, but only to refine on further details. These involved certain things the headmistress, Mrs McIntyre (she had never really been married, but it was better to be advertised as conversant with that state) had told her, from young Lady Orde's own initial confidences, artless at first, in fact bewildered, as all young properly reared brides were following on marriage. The confidence involved mention of certain Chinese powders Sir Phelim was in the habit of taking after Sunday luncheon, when they had returned in their steamer, and the results by teatime. It wasn't a suitable thought to entertain in church, but a possible combination, perhaps at Hogmanay when the minister allowed himself a glass of whisky, of the obtained powders, a sight of Nancy Purdie in some beguiling attitude to be decided on later, and the removal of poor Amy to bed with oneself on some excuse or other also to be worked out, made a combined stratagem of almost military expertise which might come off, and if it didn't no harm was done; but there was the story of that woman who'd stuffed pillows down herself some years ago in the West End of Glasgow, pretending she was expecting a further addition to an already large and respectable family, while one of the daughters had mysteriously developed consumption upstairs and was seen by nobody for nine months, by which time she had a new little brother, and was suddenly better. It might do, if only Mrs Swords was off the premises by New Year.

* * *

In extenuation of Mrs McKitterick's fancies, she herself had had an unsatisfactory marriage. Amy's papa—it was astonishing that he'd managed to produce even Amy—had ended by throwing himself under a railway train. Fortunately it had happened in Manchester, and in any case was one more thing not spoken of. Uncle Julius, of course, had had to be informed, and thereafter had made her and Amy a small allowance. By now, no doubt anyone who considered the matter at all must conclude that Amy herself had arrived in the world by parthenogenesis. Mrs McKitterick rose with others for the paraphrase, sang loudly in her strident voice, then settled again with comfort on the maroon felt padding of the manse pew. She was, to all intents, after all the minister's wife herself as far as arranging or organising anything went, despite the lingering and tactless presence of Mrs Swords. Poor Amy could never host a church soirée by herself, or even order enough calico for the missions with any economy. In fact, it had no doubt been the prospect of having her, Louisa, as his housekeeper that had induced Mr McPhail to agree to the notion of marrying Amy that time at Kilbeg after the death of his own much older sister Jessie, who had formerly seen to every matter except one. He was above thoughts of money, having a mind fixed on higher things. This in itself would have made Louisa consider him.

* * *

Aeneas McPhail had in fact watched his sister die without noticing, as he had been thinking at the time about the Book of Ezekiel. Its images and phrases fascinated him particularly with their touch of the bizarre, taking him a long day's march away from Kilbeg, where he had been by then in his charge for some time, and which, though pleasant enough with its shingled beach, mild air and a scattering of houses for retired gentlefolk up on the hill above the clachan itself, made no great demands on the intellect Mr McPhail knew, without conceit, that he possessed. At times, indeed, the sight of the old ladies in the congregation had reminded him disastrously of a flock of sheep, obediently worshipping, but without a stimulating idea in their collective heads. Jessie had long ago chased away all the young ones. The only exception was poor little Amy McKitterick, who never seemed to be free of her mother. In any case she was a colourless creature and did not bring on the urges of the flesh from which, now and again and reprehensibly, Mr McPhail knew himself to suffer. St Paul had said it was better to marry than to burn, and no doubt, but for Jessie, he himself might have married long ago; but with one thing and another he hadn't, and now he was forty-two. Before Jessie looked after him their mother had done so, and both he and they were alike in that they had a strain of fierce MacGregor blood, heavy eyebrows, great physical strength and an equally reproachful, and unsleeping, sense of sin. His father, whom Aeneas barely remembered, had been a blacksmith, and perhaps he himself would have liked to bend over an anvil with the fire blown cherry-red, and deal with horses; but his mother had said he was to be a minister, had saved every penny and taken in lodgers, with Jessie's help, after his father died, and had seen to it that he, Aeneas, worked hard enough at school to win a place at the University, and that was that. His mind, granted, had felt the benefit.

On the day in question, Jessie had gone out as usual to the beach with her knitting, the household tasks being done and his own high tea on the stove, cooking as usual. He knew she would be back in time to serve it, the Highland maid having gone off at three o'clock; they shared her with Mrs McKitterick along the way, which saved money for all parties. McPhail had seated himself in his leather armchair at the window and had taken up the lighter of two Bibles, reading the marked passages he had already prepared, and had observed Jessie settled in her usual place with her back against a particular low rock on the shore. From where he was he could see she had got with her pins to the middle of a row; she was never idle, saying, as their mother had done, that Satan found work for useless hands to do. The minister lost himself, therefore, in Ezekiel, much later on looking up to see that Jessie was still in the middle of the same row, which wasn't like her. Her grey-black hair—she was twenty years older than he was—blew about in a helpless unaccustomed fashion beneath her plain tied bonnet, and she didn't raise a hand to tidy away the strands. It wasn't like her, but he didn't start to worry immediately; she was probably thinking about something, like himself. It was not till he smelt the potatoes she'd left on the stove burning that he began to realise something was wrong; and at the same time the raised voice of the Highland maid, who was going home by way of the shore and had already noticed more than he had.

'Ochone, ochone, poor Miss McPhail iss no more, the soul, no more!'

It was a coronach he would never forget. He hastened down to the beach, sent for the doctor, helped the latter carry Jessie's body in the end back into the house, by which time various folk had assembled, among them Mrs McKitterick, who seemed at once to take charge, even to winding up the ball of knitting and sticking in the pins. His tea was irretrievably burnt, which was the least of it; Mrs McKitterick sent him round a plate later on of what she called cold supper. He ought not have been in a state to eat it, but he was hungry by then, and there would be nobody but the weeping Highland girl, if she came at all, to get his breakfast.

* * *

Miss Jessie McPhail had been buried with all solemnity, and everyone agreed that it had been a pleasant way to go, watching the Clyde ships go up and down the firth, with her knitting in her hands; and that she was certainly in heaven. Of that her brother had no reasonable doubt; Jessie had worked all her life for other folk, for his mother and for himself. He didn't know if she had ever wanted to marry; no one had thought of it. Now, he had to think what to do about himself; like most men, he was incapable of boiling an egg, and there were other things that needed a good housekeeper. Mrs McKitterick made herself invaluable in this way, coming in every day along with the Highland girl, leaving her daughter at home. That was a house, he knew, that she'd rented in Kilbeg for some years now, having come, he believed, from Manchester. More he did not ask, but instead asked her one day if she would keep house for him permanently. He could pay her a little, he said hesitantly. He hadn't been sure whether to venture it or not; she was certainly a lady, though of formidable appearance like Jessie had been, which made him feel somewhat at home. Also, she was an excellent cook and his house, under her supervision, remained clean, a fact Mr McPhail failed to notice and never had.

Louisa had demurred meantime. It was a question, she said, of Amy. If she brought her there would be gossip, and it wouldn't do to leave her always alone. 'She may perhaps expect a little money when an uncle dies; I have never left her a prey to fortune-hunters.'

He could never, come to that, remember

who it was that had suggested that he and Amy marry. It was probably not the kind of thing he would have thought of for himself.

*　　*　　*

The ceremony took place. It was in Glasgow, and quiet because of the mourning for the bridegroom's sister. The bride's great-uncle, in the north, had not come down to give her away, but sent ten pounds and good wishes. Afterwards the couple returned to the hotel where they had spent the night, the difference being that this time, Amy's mother, who of course stayed on, kissed Amy on the cheek, told her to do exactly as Mr McPhail said, and indicated the door of his room instead of her own as previously. On the following morning she greeted them, smilingly, at breakfast and remarked that it was going to be a fine day. Conversation proceeded as usual, Mr McPhail having in case little to contribute as a rule. Amy said nothing. She was in a state of bewildered terror, but one evidently didn't mention what had happened. It was one more thing that wasn't spoken of.

CHAPTER TWO

As time passed, and after the return to Kilbeg, McPhail was glad enough that he had married. Amy was submissive, caused no trouble and did not, like her mother who of course kept house as before, expect conversation. In fact he never said an unkind word to Amy, as he seldom said anything at all: the situation was taken for granted. At the beginning, it had been an agreeable surprise to sense his own large parts thrusting without guidance up her narrow virgin's passage almost at once; and increasingly by now, as his seed flowed more strongly, so did the theology inside his head. He began to hammer out, as though his young wife's body had been an anvil, sermon after sermon of remarkable strength. It was one of these that, in the second year of the marriage, chanced to be heard by Sir Phelim Orde, himself newly widowed and returning from a visit to a Highland spa for his health, as he intended to marry again. He took note of the brilliant preacher, decided McPhail was too good for Kilbeg, and also decided to use his influence, as soon as the opportunity occurred, for some well-found church in Glasgow, though at that time Dr Swords could not be displaced from the new charge Sir Phelim had himself promoted at Oakdale. However,

Providence, as happens, saw about Dr Swords very shortly, and Sir Phelim used his casting vote to influence the selection committee. In any case the other applicants had not sounded one-tenth as obviously inspired from above. There was no real disagreement about the final choice of the Reverend Aeneas McPhail; besides, he was married, always a safeguard in the ministry; young ladies in the congregation, and their mothers, otherwise tended to have flighty ideas, seeing themselves in the place of importance. It was best, instead, to cause them to remember their own.

* * *

On the day of the famous Oakdale sermon, Nancy Purdie the between-maid had forgotten hers, although being Nancy she didn't make it obvious. Evading the glance of those two old bitches, McKitterick and Swords—she'd had her troubles with the last, but it wouldn't be long now till *she* went—and that of Holy Joe Sproat, whom she saw enough of with his bits of rubber on Monday evenings on the vestry bench, worth fourpence extra, and she'd put away quite a bit in the Savings Bank by now—Nancy feasted her eyes, as she liked to do, on what young Lady Orde was wearing and what she'd probably look like without any of it on. She was an armful, no doubt of that; the most beautiful young lady Nancy or anyone else had ever seen, and as well that old Sir Phelim who'd married her had enough money to dress her as he did, because it was worth coming to church to see. Today Lady Orde wore a wine-coloured bonnet with a pink feather, long and curling down past her bright brown ringlets to her shoulder, and she'd flung the sealskin pelisse back to give everyone in the place a treat with a near-sight of what probably lay underneath. She could be anything she liked, that one; an artist's model—Nancy had briefly done that herself, but it hadn't meant enough money—or an actress, or some great lord's fancy piece; anything, except that fat old slug's wife, having to put up with you could guess what, except that everyone knew he was past it. Nancy wondered if, despite the paddle-steamer, and the riverside palace Holy Joe had told her Sir Phelim had built, with statues and a tall clock-tower with a chiming clock from Birmingham, and a winter garden and hothouses and the clothes, it was worth it. However, Lady Orde didn't look discontented, seated there with her wine-red velvet gown showing below white, white revealed flesh, curved like a dove's, and her blue Irish eyes—they said she was descended from the kings of Ireland, but they all said that—smiling up at the minister. There was a man, now, if anyone liked; wasted on the likes of poor Mrs Amy, but he'd suit young Lady Orde well enough, they'd fit. It was odd how you knew things like that. She, Nancy, had picked up quite a lot since the mill days, just watching and listening, hearing even the minister change his ways; he'd learnt to call tea supper and dinner luncheon. Even Holy Joe could be of use in such matters, provided she'd obliged, whether or not he'd peeled off his bit of rubber first. All that had started when he began to send for her regularly at the mill office, where he sometimes slept when things were busy. The others knew what it meant, as most of them had been themselves at least once. In the end, Holy Joe had recommended her, Nancy, to the Bath Street manse, saying she was a good worker and honest. Old Mrs Swords was like Joe himself, and liked value for money, but she got it; and Purdie, as the old woman called her, had stayed now five years. It was better than the mill, a step up. It had seemed quiet for a long time after the humming of the spools, the constant noise of the whirring machinery at the mill, morning and evening, six days a week. Now, there was only the sound of passing carriages, some of which stopped at the manse for their owners to leave cards, or even now and then to stay for a glass of madeira offered them nowadays by Mrs McKitterick. Mrs Amy never offered any by herself, and Mrs Swords waited to be invited. She'd learned that much, at least.

* * *

The service was almost over and the minister rose for the final prayer. He allowed himself, now all heads should be bowed, to take a quick look, again, in the direction of Sir Phelim's pew; it wasn't only a case of value for money. There she was, looking up at him still with her blue, blue eyes; they had long lashes seen from here. Her little white hands were still in the seal muff, ready to go; suddenly, meeting his glance, she smiled. Her teeth were milk-white, a kitten's; it was almost as if she'd bitten him, and her soft lips were red as roses, smiling, smiling.

He gave the blessing, aware that an unmentionable thing had happened; he had sustained an erection in the pulpit. Luckily the height hid it, and the black folds of his gown; but he mustn't look that way as often in future. He bade everyone depart in the time-honoured fashion, and descended with outward dignity down the pulpit steps, shown out by the beadle. Inwardly he was much shaken. Only prayer could save him. He was in fact not fully aware of how or why it had happened, only that it had. After all, she'd only smiled at him. She ought, it was true, to have had her glorious head down at the time.

* * *

The congregation filed out, the gentlemen

putting on their tall chimney hats in the porch, their wives smoothing down their narrow crinolines, crushed with long sitting. A few polite words were exchanged, certain social and business arrangements made; then everyone went to their carriages, unless they lived near.

Seumas the manse coachman had the equipage ready, and stepped down. After nodding formally to acquaintance—Mrs Swords was always formal, nobody knew her very well or ever had—the old *cailleach* in blinkers he saw climb in; then that cruel bitch of a mother, and the two sat side by side, facing the horses, leaving his sweet little Mrs Amy to face backwards beside the minister, who had not yet come out. Seumas helped her in, wishing he could kiss the colour into her little white face and bring her some happiness; but it wouldn't turn out in such a way; only, a man, whoever he might be, could dream.

He turned to the reins, and felt the minister climb in at last, and heard the two older women talking on in their harsh voices, one like gravel in a can, the other like a chain saw. His sweetheart was quiet and so was the minister; no doubt *he'd* heard enough of his own voice already, and it all had to happen again at the evening service. Seumas, his red head erect on a slim young neck beneath his livery hat, started up the horses and they moved smoothly off, other carriages mostly having gone already. Everyone was anxious to eat, and Seumas himself was hungry, having waited with the horses and, accordingly, like them, lacked sustenance. Driving, and to keep his mind off Amy and the two kinds of hunger, he reflected on what he knew of the history of the Clan McPhail. Like the MacGregors it had ended as a broken clan, with the one final male member hiding in a loch so that nothing showed above the water except his nose and mouth. The pursuers would have passed him by, but most unfortunately a gull was hovering and mistook him for a fish. He had been noticed and killed, but he must have left descendants; a pity.

*   *   *

Sir Phelim Orde and his lady had rejoined their paddle-steamer, which was chugging contentedly back down the Clyde. They had the great river almost to themselves, as there was no work today in the silent shipyards, whose vast hulls loomed untenanted; and the sole rival who might have been encountered, whose ownership of the *Isabella Napier* had given Sir Phelim competitive notions in the first place, went on Sundays to his own church at Row, walking there with his wife on his arm. As he travelled up-river daily during the week and Sir Phelim by now stayed at home, this suited both great men amicably. Sir Phelim sat for the present on deck, as it was a mild dry day, sipped the whisky from his own Perthshire distillery, and watched the beguiling sight of his wife, her brown curls ruffled by the light breeze their going had got up, while the rose-pink plume on her bonnet flaunted like a pennant, though there hadn't, now he came to think of it, been any rose-colour mentioned in heraldry. That was the kind of thing in which Phelim Orde had instructed himself over the years, having started out with hardly any education at all. It could be said, and nothing more ever was, that he came from humble beginnings. The fact made existing circumstances doubly pleasant; there was a time when he wouldn't have been sitting on the deck of his own paddle-steamer, drinking his own whisky, and watching an acquisition which might have been a young and luscious Rubens come to life.

She turned, smiled, and went back to contemplation of the river. Brabazon did not, naturally, drink whisky, nor would he have permitted her to do so; she had refused, today, a companionable glass of ratafia brought by the steward, saying she preferred to wait till luncheon. In fact, she was thinking about Mr McPhail and how handsome he was, exactly like the devil must be or he wouldn't tempt so many. They must ask him down to Crosslyon soon; today there was a dull baronet and a duller Justice of the Peace, and their wives, coming to dinner; luncheon meantime was private. Mrs McIntyre had of course taught her, at school, among other things to make polite talk as befitted a hostess; but with Mr McPhail there wouldn't be any need to say much. One need only look, and listen.

*   *   *

Very rich men do not always become very rich, and acquire knighthoods, by spectacular means. Strict application to business and an eye to the main chance play their part. These, and a certain flair and address, also the fact that he had rescued a well-known politician from a very sticky situation indeed at exactly the right moment, accounted for much of Sir Phelim's present prosperity. Also, three or four chance events in his past had shaped his destiny unpredictably. The first had been a bucket of cement, which a builder's apprentice was busy stirring with a long-handled implement in one of the new streets just off the West End when it was beginning to be thought of as a place for the genteel. Phelim himself, a boy then, had been paid a few coins to carry water, the kind of job he used to pick up if he wanted to eat. The apprentice had suddenly changed colour and fallen forward into his own bucket, and Phelim, setting down his pail, had first fished the man out—he was having an epileptic fit, his face by then covered alarmingly in putty-coloured sludge—, next had yelled for someone to come, and lastly had seized the long handle itself and continued to stir the cement, as if someone didn't it would turn hard. The builder himself had come along, had seen the unfortunate apprentice conveyed somewhere or other to be seen to, and had taken note of Phelim as a level-headed lad who could be relied on in emergencies. In the end he had been given the sick man's job for the time being, and by the time the man came back had made himself useful in enough ways for the old builder, who was a Highlander come down from the glens in the hard times himself, to keep him on.

Orde learned all aspects of the building trade, and having been taught to read, write and cipher earlier on at the Ragged School, revealed a head for figures, used it, and was promoted. Once he put some of the money on a horse to see what happened, and the horse won. Unlike most in such situations, young Phelim did not proceed to lose the money on the next horse and then the next and the next; he put the winnings instead into stocks and shares, which rose. In the meantime he had been taken to live, as a kind of secretary, in the Highland builder's own house in the High Street, in the old part of town, where the university students could be seen coming and going in their familiar gowns; Phelim made an acquaintance with some of them, was allowed to borrow books, and in his spare time educated himself in such ways as might offer. One other way was by means of his hostess, the builder's Glasgow-born wife, who took a fancy to him almost as a son, for the time being at least. Phelim never knew why; he was a realist and knew he wasn't handsome, though he had a certain persuasion, and his teeth had never been good. (By now, they were undoubted porcelain.) By now, also, he was the widower of the builder's widow, who on the death of her old husband had asked him to marry her, as otherwise there would be talk if Phelim stayed on in the house; at least, she pretended that was it.

'I'll see ye right, lad, if ye'll take on an old woman and do the like.' He had never forgotten the sight and sound of her, seated there in her chair, her vast form in bombazine and a culza-lamp spluttering beside her on a table with a chenille cloth and bobbles. He had never thought of her as anything but motherly, but after they were married found that her demands were far other, excessive, and almost more than he could manage, even then, young as he was. Over the years she had drained him, which accounted for the fact that, although early on he had ventured into insurance with success, also by degrees rebuilding and selling the beautiful and soot-grimed old houses of the erstwhile tobacco lords with profit—he had noted their reflected proportions and pediments almost from the cement-stirring days—and among other investments had taken major shares in the cotton-mill part owned by Joseph Sproat, he had not enough breath left to avail himself, even now and again, of the bandy-legged young mill lasses, as Sproat did, let alone savour the delectable Nancy Purdie, who from the beginning could be assessed by both of them as beyond the common run. His demanding wife took all he had in such ways, and she lived on and on; in fact, the most debatable enterprise Orde had ever ventured upon, the Oakdale development, had been worked out on paper before Lily Orde suffered a heart attack, then another, then at last the funeral. By that time he himself had bent the knee before the Queen and Prince Albert at Windsor, but had been allowed to leave Lily at home.

Home by now was a different matter by far. He had long ago moved out of the High Street house, selling it reasonably to the University authorities, then had lived on in the new West End with Lily till she died, already, as before, having sketched out on paper his heart's dream; a Clydeside mansion, with turrets and hothouses and a view of the firth, and a rose garden and winter garden, and above all a tall central tower in which a brass and enamel clock, like they'd had at the Great Exhibition, should sit and tick, tock away the hours, and chime, with a great echoing pervasive sound, those and the quarters.

Now, he was going home to Crosslyon; and not with Lily, but with Brabazon. There was only one fly in the ointment of his satisfaction with his lot these days; and one had to keep trying. They'd try again, as happened most Sundays, after luncheon.

*   *   *

Brabazon Orde, almost two years married by now, had been the star pupil at Mrs McIntyre's famous seminary for young ladies in the West End of Glasgow, which was in fact a marriage market, though nobody said so. She had been glimpsed by Sir Phelim, who of course was one of the governors, at the annual Open Day, when the young ladies who were about to be presented at the Assembly Rooms, a vast structure built in the classical style in cream Giffnock stone off Sauchiehall Street, displayed their talents as expressed in beadwork, woolwork, painting on velvet, shells glued on wooden boxes, framed samplers with an alphabet and an improving motto to be hung on the walls of their establishments when they married and settled down, and other such horrors. Mrs McIntyre, who had an original mind, had given the young ladies leave to embellish their plain dun-coloured dresses—these had a becoming shoulder-cape of the same colour for church, with braid which was also to be seen on the matching bonnets—with whatever they liked in order to show themselves to best advantage after several years of genteel education in everything but what was really necessary, as one of course expected to have servants when established.

Brabazon had avoided the bits of ribbon and feathers and fripperies and Nottingham lace laid out by the headmistress for everyone's choice, and had simply gone out to the small square garden and reprehensibly picked two daffodils, pinning one in her hair and the other at her breast. Attired thus, she made everyone else look like something off a pedlar's tray. She had a full bosom and tiny waist—there must, Mrs McIntyre had long ago decided, be Spanish blood there from the Peninsular wars—a queenly walk, like nobody else's, and small white hands which played the harp with ferocity and expertise. So wild was the music that Mrs McIntyre had not encouraged dear Brabazon's undoubted talents in that direction; a harp should be a polite social asset, not an instrument of war. Brabazon—her first name was Clara, and the whole thing had come from an Irish grandmother who in her own day had been a celebrated beauty—had a certain independence of mind which must not, or not till she was married, be allowed free rein. Having said she loathed Clara and would rather it wasn't used, this was permitted; but otherwise Brabazon was made to toe the line. It was not that there was any money, though her looks would certainly find her a husband; an aunt, not particularly interested, had sent her here, saying her niece's education would be paid for and she should be brought out; after that, she must fend for herself. Mrs McIntyre knew compassion; the child had no parents alive, and if marriage did not transpire for some reason, there was no alternative but the fate of a governess; and Mrs McIntrye had been one in her day and knew exactly what they had to endure. She was most grateful to Sir Phelim Orde for having rescued her, some years ago now, from this fate, setting her up in what had become a most celebrated and successful establishment; the merchant families of Glasgow had sent their daughters thankfully, glad to see them knowledgeably refined, and paying the fees handsomely and on time.

When, accordingly, Sir Phelim asked for a private word, which turned out to be an immediate proposal for the white hand of Brabazon, Mrs McIntyre could do no other than promote his suit. Brabazon, approached, had been unwilling at first, saying she wanted to go to the Assembly Rooms and dance, with her card filled up with a gold pencil by handsome and, so far, totally imagined young men. She had in fact been allowed to know none, as the girls were strictly chaperoned even on their weekly expedition to church. Of late, since the marriage, this had, of course, been to Oakdale, which was somewhat far from school; but carriages had been made available, as an extra.

Meantime Brabazon was persuaded that a governess's life was incurably dull and, as the headmistress expressed it, much put upon; spoilt children could be cruel, and in winter in a freezing schoolroom she herself had been made to wait till the very last before the ceremonial hot potato, sent up daily from the kitchens on purpose to warm the children's hands, had been contemptuously handed to her, stone cold at last, having been passed all round the table where they were busied otherwise with arithmetic. Perhaps it was the thought of the arithmetic, at which she was not very good, which persuaded Brabazon to become tractable; or possibly it was the description of what life would be like with Sir Phelim, who although not handsome, and many years her senior, was very, very rich. 'There is nothing in the world he will not give you if you ask,' concluded the excellent preceptress, having raised images of velvet dresses, muffs, sables, jewels, a harp of her own to play as she chose, the title, and above all the magnificent mansion lately completed on the Clyde, with its view of the mountains and the firth, and ships passing. 'There will be a far more brilliant social life there than can be found at the Assembly,' said Mrs McIntyre, 'and you need never do a hand's turn; there are enough servants for everything, including a housekeeper.' She knew all this from gossip rather than reality, but had made certain of the facts; she always did.

Other facts had however not been made clear, any more than they had to poor Amy McPhail. Men liked their brides innocent; and innocence had been preserved to a surprising degree among every one of Mrs McIntyre's young ladies.

*   *   *

The wedding took place the week before the Assembly ball, to which Sir Phelim had determined his betrothed should on no account go. He had no illusions about his own appearance, he'd put on weight with the years, and the prospect of watching Brabazon in the arms of various young men—the waltz had daringly been included in Mrs McIntyre's curriculum—was not to be expected of him by now. He sent, as a present on the day before the ceremony, the most expensive bonnet in Glasgow, specially delivered in a beribboned box the shape of a tub of treacle. As a prospect of the delights to come it was a harbinger; Brabazon made an enchanting appearance in it as a no longer particularly unwilling bride. Sir Phelim had already promised her the harp as well. The aunt was present at the ceremony, relieved that the considerable expense involved had at last paid off. So, both as business associate and groomsman, his fair hair smoothed and darkened with macassar oil, was Holy Joe Sproat.

*   *   *

All that had been almost two years ago. Since then life had settled into its pattern, and Sir Phelim no longer went daily up to town, but worked from his office at Crosslyon; everything else could be left to good, reliable Sproat to handle. The steamer docked as usual at the jetty, the Ordes got off, walking up arm-in-arm to the main gate and the lodge. Beyond, the completed clock tower reared, and as they proceeded across the raked garden paths the great chime rang out for the hour. Luncheon would of necessity be late, and light; but there would be dinner to which to look forward this evening.

During luncheon, which was served on Minton plates specially designed for Sir Phelim with a view of the completed Crosslyon mansion itself in a delicately engraved dark oval on the sides, Sir Phelim could be observed to take out a small phial of greyish powder and sprinkle a pinch of it on his cold ham. This, as was understood, was his medicine, and afterwards he put the stoppered phial back without comment. Following fruit and coffee he suggested that they go upstairs. Brabazon rose, and obeyed silently. She hadn't said much during the meal. What came next happened most Sundays, and was the part she liked least. It had started after a lack of anything happening at all in the first few weeks of marriage. By now, she had an idea of what ought to have done, but it still hadn't. She was sorry for Sir Phelim, who seemed to take it greatly to heart; she would have helped in some way if she could. In fact the chief trouble was getting used to the great clock in the tower, which Sir Phelim had had specially installed after seeing one like it at the Great Exhibition some years ago with his first wife. It had an extremely loud tick, and that and the chimes went on all night. It had taken some time to get used to it, and at the same time she'd got used to Sir Phelim. She was fond of him and he was kind to her; she'd never had as many dresses.

She undressed now, as was expected of her; and lay down naked, except for her silk stockings and garters, on the bed. This was a large four-poster in which Brabazon slept at night by herself. It had silk curtains embroidered in exotic colours in India, trimmed with pale knotted fringe. She would gaze up at them and listen to the ticking clock while Sir Phelim tried again for some time to do whatever it was he couldn't. His hands pried and stroked, fingered, caressed; there wasn't a part of her he didn't touch, sooner or later; she heard his desirous gruntings, felt his thrusting weight upon her, the flaccid belly—he didn't walk much now—overflowing her on either side. Like the clock, she'd got used to it. The only thing that disturbed her was that, after some time, sensations were aroused in her that couldn't be satisfied by Sir Phelim, whatever he did. His panting had, by now, turned to sobs, like a child's. She tried to comfort him as best she could, but by this time her eyes were closed against the unbidden urges. It was almost as though she were on fire, and there were nobody to put it out. Sir Phelim was kissing her all over as usual, and had ended up crying on her stomach. If she had known, in his mind were the terrible curses from Leviticus. *If your vines bear fruit, worms will eat the grapes.*

He found himself saying it aloud. 'I didn't know worms liked grapes,' Brabazon said. He began to laugh then, almost as though he wasn't sad any more.

'That kind of thing is partly why I love you, my dear,' he said. *My beloved is the only one of her mother; her breasts are like two young roes that feed among the lilies.* He didn't say that aloud, as things were. Instead he said, as if nothing had gone wrong, 'It is time now to dress ourselves for dinner, I believe. Ye will wear the sapphires, eh? The guests who are coming must be shown them, and yourself.'

He rose then and went to his dressing room, where he slept at nights. He hadn't ever explained why, but she knew he didn't like her seeing his false teeth, steeping in their bowl, or the chamber-pot. She had one of her own in the decorated Minton china, and a maid called Phemie who would help her dress. Yes, she would wear the sapphires.

It had already occurred to her, during proceedings, that if it had been Mr McPhail, he wouldn't have had to use his finger once or twice. She couldn't have told how she knew.

*   *   *

Phemie the maid moved about the room quietly afterwards, smoothing the fringed bed ready for night and tidying away her ladyship's day-clothes. It was always a pleasure to hang them alongside the rest in the great mahogany cupboards, opening their doors to the sweet scent of dried lavender from the kitchen garden, which hung in muslin bags among the silks and velvets to keep them from getting stale; not that my lady had the unpleasant odour some ladies were given to, she was as fresh as a rose. Phemie gave a last admiring glance at the rails of gowns, shook out a whalebone crinoline frame and bestowed it. The fashion-plates her ladyship kept on a side-table said they were getting wider in Paris, and how would the French ladies get through doorways there? Whatever was fashionable, Sir Phelim would see that her ladyship wore it, even if he had to widen the Crosslyon doors; it was well seen he doted on her.

Phemie laid out, before going down for her supper in the servants' hall, the delicate nightwear her ladyship would wear for bed; a filmy nightgown trimmed with Brussels lace, and a matching negligée for when she sat at the dressing-table to have her hair brushed out. It was done a different way this evening, for the dinner-party; scooped up in a great shining knot at the back of my lady's head, to show off the swinging sapphire earrings. A treat she'd looked in that dark-blue satin dress by the time she was ready; and everything to be put away again, the long brown curling hair brushed out a hundred times, before the seventeen-hour day ended. It was a pleasant situation and Phemie had no complaints. After supper, as the gentlefolk were still in the dining-room and there would be music upstairs afterwards, the maid took the chance to put her feet up. As might have happened with the late Miss McPhail and had not. Satan found work for idle hands to do, and she, Phemie Denny, should be knitting herself a pair of stockings she'd started. However, it was allowable to doze off for a while, so long as she was awake when rung for: and that would not be quite yet. Phemie slumbered in her chair, until the expected sound of her ladyship's little silver bell should come. It hung on a ribbon by the wall, above the table with the fashion-plates. The ribbon was embroidered by hand in France with roses and violets, and kept the bell from getting mislaid.

The guests had arrived. The Justice of the Peace was a small perky man and the baronet a tall thin one. Their wives were inversely proportionate and they all lived near Loch Lomond. Brabazon received them in the best traditions of Mrs McIntyre; behind her, a life-sized portrait of her in the sapphires and the blue dress, recently painted by order of Sir Phelim, hung on the wall at the far end of the long shining mahogany dining-table, set as it was with gleaming silver and shining crystal, flowers—she'd helped to arrange those for a moment, at least—and candles in tall sconces. Outside, the river shone as well, with lights from the farther shore. Everyone talked, ate and drank politely; the wine was special, from Sir Phelim's deep cellars, selected by him yesterday with care. Afterwards the ladies—the J.P.'s wife was from Glasgow, the up-and-coming end, which made her accent uncomfortable to listen to—withdrew to leave the men to their port, and upstairs the harp waited. The J.P.'s wife offered to sing. Brabazon sat down, and the good lady asked if she could perhaps play songs from Thomas Moore, to accompany one?

As it happened, Brabazon knew them from school; and the one first chosen, *The Harp that Once,* had always aroused fierce emotion in her. It was her Irish blood, no doubt. She had already noticed that the blonde frizzed lady about to sing—her name was Mrs Smillie—fell into the common error of talking about *may* husband, and feared for the Harp. Her fears were realised; having struck the strings and played an opening arpeggio, she was afflicted with 'The Hairp that Wince through Taira's *Hells*,' in a rasping soprano, and couldn't stand it. When it came to the second verse, and the harsh reedy voice stopped for instants to draw breath, Brabazon joined in spontaneously with her own rich mezzo. Aunt Dorothy hadn't agreed to pay for singing lessons at Mrs McIntyre's, they were one more extra, but Brabazon knew well enough that she herself could sing like a thrush in a lilac tree.

No more to kings and ladies bright
The harp of Tara swells;
The only chord that wakes at night
The tale of ruin tells;

Thus Freedom now so seldom wakes;
The only sob she gives
Is when some heart indignant breaks,
To show that still she lives!

The two voices, soaring in unequal competition, dwindled to one as the gentlemen came in, till Brabazon was left singing alone, the foe having retreated, mortified. There came a great, final sweeping chord on the harp strings. The J.P's wife had bridled, then fallen silent.

* * *

'I think yon Mrs Smillie was maybe a wee bit offended,' Sir Phelim told his wife reproachfully afterwards. 'I didn't know ye were so fine a singer, my dear. We must send ye for lessons, the best teacher that can be found.' He beamed proudly after all, his eyes bloodshot from the port.

There was an Italian lady in Glasgow, she knew, who was very expensive, but he wouldn't grudge anything. She leaned over and kissed him, and said she was sorry if Mrs Smillie had had her feelings hurt. 'I couldn't bear the way she said the words. It's an Irish song. She isn't the right person to sing them.'

'Well, they'll all know by now that ye can sing, at any rate. Ye will be asked to other folks' houses for it, I doubt not.' He looked at her with longing, unable to be angry as most men would have been; how superb she was in his sapphires, shining as they did at her snowy throat and in her ears, and the bracelet on her shapely white arm, raised as it had been to pluck the harp's strings gracefully! He had a perfect possession in her, if only—Well, he would keep trying as regarded that; all his life he had persevered, perseverance was his motto. Meantime, he would arrange for Brabazon's singing lessons. It would mean her going up to town once a week as well as Sundays. Depending on pressures of business as they came, he might accompany her or else not.

He heard, through his plans, the tower clock chiming midnight. The guests had left more than an hour ago, with Mrs Smillie in the huff.

CHAPTER THREE

'I think that I will go to lie down for a little while, Mama,' had said Amy about half-past two that same day. The minister had gone to his study, and they were in the drawing-room with Mrs Swords. It was not correct to have any occupation on the Sabbath, which made it an ideal day for callers; but today there were none, and she did not look forward to the next two hours with nothing to do or say.

Louisa replied that no doubt Mrs Swords would excuse her. Amy wilted a little at the implied rebuke, but escaped. Louisa allowed her to go, as she wanted in any case to sound the widow on the general matter of Nancy Purdie, who had after all been in her employment when one came. Also, there was no interesting reason why Amy should want to lie down; her mother kept a sharp eye on her periods, and there had been one quite recently, though they tended to be irregular. Altogether Amy was not, as Uncle Julius would have put it, a winner at long odds. Purdie would be more reliable. Louisa turned to the widow and tried to elicit information, without much success, Mrs Swords merely said she never asked too much, as few servants had any morals nowadays, and provided they carried out their tasks adequately, it was as much as one could expect. She added that Mr Sproat the session-clerk had recommended Purdie, who had formerly and for some time been employed at his mill. Since coming she had given satisfaction.

Amy meantime had decided not, after all, to go and lie down on her bed. If Mr McPhail came in, he might forget it wasn't night-time; that had happened once before, when he was thinking about the next sermon, at least she supposed so. His thrustings left her exhausted and drained; it didn't hurt by now so much as at the beginning, but she would still rather it didn't have to happen. Somewhere else, anywhere to be private, would do instead; but there were only two places. One was the lavatory, where she could hardly lock herself in all afternoon. The other—

Amy found herself stealing down the back stairs. In the kitchen there was no clatter today of washing up, no one was there to see her pass. She let herself quietly out of the yard door, crossed the yard itself, seeing the shreds of straw blowing in the light wind; their presence meant the carriage had been swept out and polished yesterday. A Sabbath silence still prevailed as she moved past the horses' stalls to where the uncoupled carriage itself reared, black, shining and prosperous, its hood down as there hadn't been rain lately. Amy climbed in, settled herself on the floor and drew her knees up, wrapping her skirts close.

She was hidden from everyone. It was a sensation she had hardly ever known; always, there had been Mama watching, answering for her, not letting her be herself. Who was she? Everyone must think her stupid; she never had anything to say, it was always said already. Perhaps—the state of being what Mama called unwell, and Mr McPhail unclean, hadn't come till she was seventeen, and Mama had formerly said if it didn't come by the time you were sixteen you went off your head—perhaps she was really off hers, not like other people. The thought made Amy want to laugh, then cry. She found herself sobbing quietly, her cheek against the rim of the carriage seat on which they'd all driven up this morning.

There was somebody there after all; somebody whose red hair flamed in the light from the archway now his livery hat was off. He was in shirt-sleeves; he couldn't have been expecting anyone. She felt him kneel down beside her and put his arm about her. It was comforting; Mama would have been shocked, as he was a servant. Amy didn't care.

'Why are you crying, *m'eudail*? Have they been unkind to you?' He spoke in Gaelic.

Amy suddenly realised that she didn't really know what kindness was. Everybody else thought first of themselves, even Mama. Mama had made her marry Mr McPhail; left to herself she wouldn't have, especially now she knew what happened in bed. If only—

It was her mother, he was thinking, the bitch; and that *pulaidh* her husband, taking his rights most likely without considering her at all. He himself would show her, now, what love was; he had after all loved her for a long time. Gently, thoughtfully, slowly, he began to caress her; hearing her sobbing cease and change, become at last a contented moaning; a new innocence; discovery came with the kissing of her mouth, her breast. His hands were gentle, as they were with the horses; animals trusted him, so did she, soon, very soon. She heard him murmur love-words in Gaelic, some she had not known; words whose meaning could be guessed at by the sounds they made, like water running over pebbles, like the wind on a moor in spring. It was as though she was transported out of her plain flat body to become changed, a goddess; she had never known glory and fulfilment until now. She heard herself at last cry out against him, savouring the intimate warmth of his eager, loving young flesh.

'Hush, now, hush, *sámhaich,* they must not hear, must never know. I will not forget, nor will you. It is different now for both of us from what has been. You must go soon; it is time for the service, they will be looking for the carriage. You know that I am here always, that you are mine and I am yours, and no other's. *Beannachd, gabh tlachd ann.*'

* * *

Callers had come to the drawing-room after all, the preceptor and his wife, a plain pleasant creature in an India shawl. She was expecting their third child, and Louisa McKitterick thought how similar a pillow would look to that situation; tomorrow, she would go down to Oakdale in the carriage, and talk to Purdie in private, without fear of interruption. She knew exactly what to say, and how much money to offer; not too much, not too little. She stood up to say farewell to the guests; and saw, out of the window, Amy returning to the house from outside, without her bonnet. The child looked flushed, perhaps she had gone straight out after lying down. One would enquire. 'How are the dear children?' she said to the precentor's wife, without listening to how they were. Their carriage bowled away presently.

* * *

'Amy dear, you should always put on a bonnet and shawl to go outside. Why were you out? Were you visiting the stables?' There could be no other destination, after all, through the yard.

Amy said she had remembered leaving something in the carriage that morning. 'What was it?' enquired the indefatigable Louisa, more from habit than interest.

'My handkerchief.' It was astonishing how easily one could tell lies.

'Did you find it?' It hadn't been lying about in the carriage this morning; she would have noticed. Then she noticed another thing, Amy's bodice was wrongly buttoned up, so that the ruffles which always had to be sewn inside, to correct her skimpiness, showed a little. It certainly had not been like that earlier for church. No doubt dear Amy had begun to loosen her clothing before lying down, and had then done things up again in a hurry. It was the kind of detail one remembered, for some reason.

Amy said vaguely that she hadn't found the handkerchief, it must be somewhere else. 'Well, go now to tidy yourself for the evening drive,' said Louisa, 'and be careful, another time, to dress properly when beyond the house. Such things are spoken about if seen, and you have a position to keep up.'

Amy heard her as if from another planet. Nothing could take away the bliss of what had happened, nothing. He was within her for always, and she was in him, having given herself utterly in a way she could never have begun to imagine. To look at the back of his head this evening, driving her with the rest, would be different from all other times. Everything, as he'd said, was altogether different from now on.

*   *   *

Next day, Mrs McKitterick announced her intention of going down to Oakdale in the carriage after luncheon, to inspect the state of the pews. 'You will stay, Amy, and help Mrs Swords with the missionary calico.' The minister, she added, would be dropped off at the Infirmary, for his visits, and would no doubt walk back.

Amy felt disappointment that she wouldn't be able, once again as yesterday evening, to watch Seumas' red head on its long neck, and his hands as he drove, and perhaps have a word with him while Mama was inside the church. However, she obeyed as usual; nothing, even yet, could take away the happiness she still felt, and last night Mr McPhail hadn't touched her, having, it was evident, something else on his mind. Amy had pretended to be asleep, but instead had stayed awake with her eyes closed for a long time, remembering.

She remembered still, while sewing small neat stiches in the ugly calico. With the new kinds of thought that had lately come, she told herself boldly that the heathen would look much better without it. However, one didn't say such things to Mrs Swords. That lady, still in her black crape weepers, talked now and again between spells of silence. She would say unexpected things, or none at all. Amy recalled that Mama had said she was very well connected. She must have been handsome once, as far as one could judge beneath the mourning. Dr Swords had been a famous preacher in his day.

As though the widow had known Amy's thoughts, she spoke. 'I have been married twice,' Mrs Swords said. 'On the first occasion it was for my husband's money, and on the second for his mind. I have buried them both, and now I am going back to England.'

Amy was surprised; Mama, who had been hoping this would happen, hadn't said anything about it. She murmured something accordingly, still a trifle overawed by the weepers. They hung down on either side of Mrs Swords' face, like—like a horse's blinkers. The widow answered equably.

'I have not told your mother; you may do so if you wish. It is yourself, and not Mrs McKitterick, who is the mistress of the manse; she takes too much for granted. She will no longer, at least, make use of my coachman; I intend taking him with me. He has better hands with a horse than any man I have employed hitherto. I intend raising his wages.'

Amy felt her inner glow subside and crumble to ashes; her face whitened. She saw her own hands stitch, stitch on at the coarse, provided stuff; this would be her life from now, this and—and Mr McPhail. It occurred to her then that perhaps Seumas could refuse to go; could he, would he? Would Mr McPhail allow him to stay, thereby offending Dr Swords' powerful widow? Would Mama take Seumas' part?

She remembered that Mrs Swords had lately said she, Amy, was the mistress of the manse. Perhaps she could arrange something, think of something. The pleasure of the day, of being alive, had however gone. *You know that I am here always.* Soon, he might not be.

* * *

Mrs McKitterick, duly driven down to the parish church, took less heed of Seumas' red head than of Sir Phelim Orde's new red sandstone flats, very expensive, one understood, and lived in by persons appreciative of quality. Louisa herself had been asked to tea, with Amy, on one occasion by a well-found parishioner, and had noted the grandeur of the inner close steps, four flights high and scrubbed milk-white by houseproud occupants; one eccentric lady was said to polish the brass knobs all the way down the mahogany balustrade herself, as she said the maids didn't do it properly. Sir Phelim must have made a great deal of money out of the enterprise; once one had enough to start with, there was of course no limit to what one could do. Had she herself been younger, and had

Uncle Julius's fortune been available, she might well have thought of various such schemes; not all women were as incapable as men had evidently decided.

With this thought as they had arrived, Seumas handed Amy's mother politely down; and it occurred to her, or might have done, that here was a young man, after all, and had it been anyone but Amy who was unexpectedly at the carriage yesterday afternoon, one might have feared, perhaps . . . and yet, no, not with a servant. In any case, a second presence obtruded itself at that precise moment and caused Mrs McKitterick's mind to alter its sights at least for the time. Sproat the session-clerk was coming unobtrusively out of the side door which led to the vestry, his hat on his head. While his appearance might have several reasonable explanations, Louisa had a certain feeling in her bones; she'd always felt it, the man was like a cock-sparrow; she disliked him, but it was of course not polite to make the fact plain. Louisa bowed in formal fashion, Holy Joe lifted his tall hat briefly and walked on, and Mrs McKitterick betook herself inside; the door, of course, was unlocked meantime as it was cleaning day.

Purdie was to be seen at once, and had her skirts and her apron bundled up, while she twisted something furtively in the top of her stocking. It all bore out the feeling Louisa already had in her bones, and at the same time made her future plans clearer, a very little, at the edges. On the other hand it might perhaps make them less so. One must see. 'What are you doing?' she asked sharply. 'I saw Mr Sproat leave a moment ago.'

Nancy said she was tightening her garter. 'That is not the case,' said Louisa, who had eyes in her head. 'That is money you were twisting in your stocking. Has there been impropriety with Mr Sproat? Answer me truthfully, if you please.'

The bench was empty, a mute witness. The minister's mother-in-law stood firm, a recording angel in jet bugles, if that was what an angel looked like. Nancy capitulated, as there was no help for it; she'd probably lost her situation as it was. She explained that it didn't do any harm to anybody. Mr Sproat wasn't a married gentleman, was always careful, and a bit of extra money was useful.

Louisa thought quickly. If the woman made a habit of it with other men, there was the risk of disease. She asked forthrightly about both matters. Nancy blushed as far as her high brave colour would allow. No, she said, there had only been this one gentleman for whom she'd begun to oblige in the office when she was at the mill. She didn't mention the artist, whom of course she'd obliged likewise while she was his model; artists expected it. He'd hung, as they called it, the painting of her afterwards in a gallery in Sauchiehall Street. It hadn't shown her face, as she'd posed combing her long hair with her arms up, as if anybody would while they were stark naked, but there it was. She hoped somebody had bought the painting to give Mac, that had been his name, a bit of money. He'd had a beard. He'd moved out somewhere beyond town now, a pity.

She became aware that Mrs McKitterick was asking her for a most astonishing favour. What was more, the pay was good; better than Holy Joe had ever handed her.

* * *

'I will not go to England with the old *cailleach*, and I have told her so. I will go to Canada, where I can make a great deal of money. When I have enough I will send for you. You will come to me there, *grádhaichte*?'

She would come; nothing would prevent her, even if she had to go in bare feet. *I would follow you through the world in a white petticoat.* Who had said that? She'd seen or heard it somewhere.

They hadn't let him stay on here, her mother and Mr McPhail. It wouldn't be courteous to Mrs Swords, they said. Mr McPhail said he would do without a coachman, it saved money. In any case she would have hated whoever came. She didn't want to say it, or for Mr McPhail to touch her again; so far, he hadn't. They were standing now, she and Seumas, at the horses' heads, and he was about to uncouple the carriage for the last time. She was having to pretend this was an ordinary goodbye, in case anyone was watching from the window. In any case Mama would call for her at any moment. 'Goodbye,' she heard herself say. There should have been a lot more said, much more.

'I will write,' he told her. 'It will be a little while, as I have to work my passage. Once there, I can find other work. Many have gone already. There is timber to be felled in the great forests, at the least. Do not forget me. I will write, as I say. They are looking now, the women in the kitchen; you do not want to be seen. Go now, my heart, *mo cridhe.* It is only for a little, till I can keep you with me always.'

She turned away, and went back to the house. Once there, it was made evident that there would be no danger of Mr McPhail's attentions for quite some time. Her mother told her she, Amy, was in the family way, and was to sleep with her in her own room meantime.

It was an invention, of course; but the minister had to be deceived, also rendered in so deprived a bodily state that he would unquestioningly take to methods used by the Old Testament patriarchs in their needs, which seldom seemed to vary. Mrs McKitterick was careful not to refer to Abraham, still less Jacob; she merely asked Mr McPhail to look up his Bible for her about something else on the same page. His eye could therefore not avoid encountering Hagar, whose mistress had been hard on her; and perhaps the name of the maidservant which for the moment escaped Louisa and who had borne a child, by request of Rachel, to Jacob on Rachel's knees. Manners and morals were quite different by now, most mercifully; but one way and another Amy, at any rate, would do what she was told as usual. It was not yet nearly time to introduce the first pillow inside Amy's ruffles.

* * *

The tumult of Mrs Swords' departure at last was over, and Amy walked through the deserted floor the former minister's widow had occupied. There was nothing left to remind anyone of the singular personage who had lived here; all mementoes of both her marriages, including a portrait, commissioned by the church authorities, of the white-haired, stern-faced old preacher seated with his tall hat laid by him, had gone. He also had been a difficult man to know, formal, they said, and a trifle chilling, though his heart had been kind enough. Amy wondered why he and the widow had married, detaining her for many years from returning south to her people. Nobody now would ever know.

She came on one item which had been left,

no doubt because it was cumbersome; the enormous bath, with multiple brass taps, not installed but merely delivered at Mrs Swords' order and expense; hot water still had to be brought up by the housemaids in cans from the kitchen boiler to fill it. Amy looked at the unused brass taps with interest; one for hot water, another for cold, others for different things including eau-de-cologne. That would be refreshing. It came, if so, from a container at the back. If only there were pipes, one could turn everything on.

The more she thought of it, the pleasanter it seemed if she could make use of these rooms for herself, and be private. To have to sleep with Mama freed her from Mr McPhail, certainly, but to be free of Mama also was becoming a need Amy felt with mounting intensity. Soon now—how she hoped it would be soon! she would hear from Seumas, and whether she was in what Mama called the family way or not, nothing would keep her from joining him; they could lose themselves together in so vast a country as Canada, and never be found. It was a dream which would once have seemed impossible of fulfilment; now, with the new strength given her, anything was possible, anything.

She became aware that she was being watched from the doorway, and turned to find the between-maid Purdie standing there, her hands twisting unusually in her apron. 'What is it?' said Amy sharply. She wasn't sharp with the servants as a rule, or with anyone, but for once she would have liked to have been left alone. Purdie was, however, good-natured, as most stout people are; she replied evenly, a smile in the dark eyes beneath her cap. Mrs McKitterick had sent, she said, to say there were visitors in the drawing-room, and Mrs McPhail's presence was required.

Why? thought Amy in her new rebellion; Mama says everything that has to be said to anyone. I only sit there. However, she went down, Purdie standing aside respectfully to let her pass. The woman took a look at Amy's figure which Amy herself failed to see. They said the minister's wife was expecting, but it didn't look like it; she was the same as she'd always been, Purdie decided, flat as a board.

There were three persons seated in the drawing-room, one Louisa herself and on the sofa, two ladies in street dress. One was the well-heeled parishioner who had invited them to tea at her Oakdale flat some weeks ago. This was no doubt a return call. She had brought with her a friend, Mrs Smillie, who lived out of town but was in today, to do a little shopping. She would return by river in the evening.

Amy took a faint dislike to Mrs Smillie, who was, it became clear, besides being over-genteel, a fount of ill-natured gossip. At present she was talking about the recent visit she and her husband—'*may* husband'—had made to Sir Phelim Orde's famous mansion down the Clyde. It was, of course, as magnificent as had been supposed, inside as well as outside; but that young wife of his was a minx. It was well seen she had married the old man for his money; what other reason could there be? 'She herself was nobody in particular,' went on Mrs Smillie, who happened to be nobody herself. 'She has a most notable opinion of her own singing voice, and interrupted one of may songs in a very rude fashion. Ay was much mortified, and did not sing again.'

'You must come and sing for us at a soirée,' put in Louisa without sincerity. Amy listened to the further denigration of Brabazon with some compassion; her dress had been far too loud, she was ablaze with jewels, too much so for a simple dinner party; and everything she did was, quite obviously, open to comment which would be spread all over Glasgow. Amy recalled having noticed the glorious Lady Orde on occasions beside old Sir Phelim in their pew, and had greatly admired her and wished she herself was one-half as beautiful. However Seumas loved her, plain Amy, as she was. The thought made her smile.

'Where were you, Amy?' enquired Louisa when the visitors had left. Amy replied that she had been looking at Mrs Swords' rooms, and would greatly like to use them for herself.

'I should particularly like a bedroom of my own,' she ventured, greatly daring. Mama in fact snored a little.

'That is not advisable in your present situation. If there should be an accident, I must be at hand.' There was also the question of Mr McPhail's continued celibacy; by now, he must be feeling the distinct lack of a partner in the marriage-bed. Next week, she would send Purdie down to the chemist; it was not as easy to obtain strong powders of any kind since Miss Madeleine Smith's notorious and successful purchases of arsenic not long ago in Sauchiehall Street. She'd said it was for rats. It was difficult now for oneself, for instance, to explain the delicate requirement for these particular grey powders; but Purdie could merely say she had been instructed to buy some for her master, and need know no more.

'You may certainly make use of the rooms during the day, Amy,' said Louisa McKitterick generously.

* * *

The Reverend Aeneas McPhail found himself in an increasingly dissatisfied state. It was not only the lack of the convenience of Amy in his bed; he admitted that she was little else to him; but in addition his sermons, which he regarded as the most important part of his ministry, were becoming almost repetitive; he could not seem to summon new ideas, and his delivery from the pulpit suffered; he was aware of a growing lack of attention in the congregation, and was likewise aware that they would be saying he had accepted the charge and, having made sure of it, had sat back and let his standards slip. In appeal and desperation, last week he had turned his head once again towards Sir Phelim's pew, as if to make sure of the support of the fountain-head at least. There sat Brabazon beside her husband, and he couldn't help looking at her again then; she was wearing, as it was summer by this time, oyster-coloured faille trimmed with narrow black bands at the hem, throat and sleeves. If anything she was more beautiful than ever; and in her blue eyes, today, there was frank appeal, as if for help from him of some kind. How willing he would be to aid her, and dared not! The result had been further misery before he left the pulpit; and no way of taking himself in hand.

He tried to interest himself in what else went on in the parish, and the mission it already supported in the poorer part of the city. Sproat was the man for that; he had organised several charities on his own account, being anxious to attract approval from the civic authorities. He collected clothing for ragged children once a year; once a month, he showed improving slides to fallen women, and seeing the minister's awakened interest invited him to attend. The women sat drably, having been reclaimed from perdition, in rows on benches in the hall hired by Sproat for such occasions. They turned their heads as Mr McPhail came in, seeing in this tall manly figure a more exciting prospect by far than the slides, which they didn't understand; what they came for was the hot cup of tea provided after Mr Sproat's impromptu prayer, with milk and sugar ready mixed from the pot. The minister went about among them, having accepted a cup of tea for himself, and tried to talk to them but didn't seem to know what to say. He was best in the pulpit, and knew it; or at least had once been. Something, he realised, would have to bring him physical and mental relief; the nights were increasingly tormenting, and he could no longer concentrate in thought.

*   *   *

He had, as Mrs McKitterick had foreseen, reminded himself of the Old Testament fathers, and recalled the fact that, in Jacob's household at least, there had been two wives, granted by an unforeseen arrangement of the father-in-law's. Abraham, apart from the venture with Hagar, had married again after burying his wife Sarah and mourning for her; it was evidently not considered good for a man to be alone, even then. The young woman's name had been Keturah, and though fertile she was not much spoken of, any more than the shady business of Abimelech and Rebekah; nothing of the latter kind would have been permitted nowadays. McPhail turned the pages almost idly, and came to the Book of Judges, which was worse; everywhere there were harlots, and Samson had been deprived of his strength in the end through a woman. What was he himself to do? He could not endure another experience like last Sunday's; he was becoming less of a man, would become less of a preacher. He began to wonder what would be the end of him. It took nine months for a child to be born. Once, in Jessie's day, he could have endured it; not now.

Louisa McKitterick had missed none of it; his temper was growing short, and she continued to protect Amy. On the other hand Hallowe'en was pending, and McPhail's recent interest in Joe Sproat's temperance involvements, supposedly to try to prevent the increasing drunkenness among the poorer classes, might surely permit him a glass of Sir Phelim's whisky on that night if she said it had been specially sent. Whisky and a grey powder combined, with Purdie sent to deliver it, her large breasts uncorseted beneath her plain stuff bodice, should serve if Aeneas McPhail was a man at all. There seemed no doubt of that, and if things were to work out equally, the sooner the better with Purdie, for whom one occasion of the kind might not, after all, be enough.

*   *   *

Hallowe'en in Glasgow was intended as a mockery of what had once been All Saints' Eve and All Souls. It was no longer *au fait* to pray for the dead, but living folk wore painted skulls and masks and carried cut-out pumpkins containing lit candles, and children thus disguised, and other than children, stopped folk in the streets demanding money. Nobody by now was certain what it was all about; it had become a tradition like other things. McPhail, who did know, shut himself in his study; and presently his grave reading was interrupted by the entrance of Purdie herself, with a glass of whisky and a bottle on a tray.

'Mistress McKitterick poured this ready for ye, minister, as it's Hallowe'en. It's Sir Phelim Orde's own whisky, he maybe sent it.' She wasn't going to tell the exact lies the old bitch had instructed her in; it had been enough to see the pinch of grey powder put by the minister's mother-in-law in good whisky. Maybe the minister himself wouldn't know the difference; he didn't often take spirits.

She moved against the desk, her comely bosom confronting him. McPhail averted his eyes, and accepted the whisky absently. Nancy would have left the tray and bottle on the desk, but he bade her take it away.

'This will be enough,' he said and returned to his reading. She didn't doubt it, but those powders, she knew already, took a little time to work. In a further half-hour she looked in again, with the bottle; would he maybe like a second glass, as it was Hallowe'en?

The aphrodisiac was churning in him; he had no further resistance. He swallowed the second glass hastily, then seized her.

*   *   *

Amy found that her mother was being less difficult than might have been expected about her use, by day, of Mrs Swords' former rooms. She had even ordered hot water to be sent up from the kitchens to try out the bath. Entering it at last, when the water was cool enough, had been pleasant; she'd even turned on the eau-de-cologne tap, and the old lady must have filled the container for herself at some time, because the ghost of scent came out. To lie in scented hot water was a treat few enjoyed, and Amy took her time over it, even daring to look down with interest at her own naked body. It was difficult to do so when Mama was present; she insisted on one's covering up to undress, as nakedness was immodest. Now, Amy decided she liked what she saw; her body was less thin and uninteresting than she'd thought, in fact her breasts—she flushed a little, the word wasn't spoken, one called it a bust when visiting the dressmaker—seemed fuller, though not as tender as they'd been a few weeks ago, when they'd chafed for a time against the ruffles sewn inside her bodice. By now, ruffles were hardly needed; and her stomach was becoming quite round.

She raised one slim pale leg in the water, watching the drops cascade from her white foot, her thin calf. Perhaps when they were in Canada, she and Seumas, there would be swimming; she'd looked at the map. There were a great many lakes, but it depended where he was. She hoped his sensitive, gentle hands were not being hurt and roughened with logging and felling timber. It could not, surely, be long now before she heard from him. If only she might hear, even to know that he was well, that he still thought of her! It wasn't possible that he could have forgotten. *You know I am there always*. Something like that.

The water was growing cold. She came out, put on her clothes after drying herself, and went down soon, feeling refreshed. It had taken more of a pull than usual to fasten her stay-laces. What the family way meant she still wasn't sure, and didn't like to ask. All she knew was that she was free to be herself because of it, and that was pleasant; and she hadn't been what Mama called unwell for quite a long time.

*   *   *

In fact, a letter had already come for Amy, who had not received it.

Aeneas McPhail had been returning from a meeting of his elders when he saw the postman come down the manse steps, having handed in the mail. The man raised his cap respectfully. One or two letters had already been placed by the housemaids on the silver tray in the hall. McPhail sorted through them, saw some for his mother-in-law and one for Amy, which was unusual; it was written in careful copperplate, and had come from Canada. He was not one of those husbands who opened their wives' mail, and having separated out his own sent the rest, by the maid, up to his mother-in-law.

Mrs McKitterick, less scrupulous, opened the letter; who could be writing to Amy?

Gradhach, it began.

This is to tell you that I have found work. It will not be long till there is enough money. For the time I am sending the directions to which to write. (There followed an address in Ontario.) *Next time, it will be better news still.* He—it was quite evidently, from the signature, a he—remained her ever devoted James Macrae.

Louisa did not know much Gaelic; the meaning of *gradhach* could only be guessed at. For instants she was in a state of bewilderment; what had happened in Amy's carefully supervised life that could have led to the arrival of such a letter? She then recalled that the Gaelic for James was Seumas, pronounced Shamus, and that he had been the former coachman; and there had been that unaccountable visit of Amy's one day to the stables, though it might, after all, still mean less than one by now feared. This letter, evidently written with care lest it should be read, might well have said far more; why was such a person—they learned to write very correctly indeed in schools in the Highlands, the dominies were strict—writing to Amy at all? Perhaps she herself should ask; and yet as things were—and they were going very satisfactorily with Purdie and Mr McPhail—perhaps not. Purdie had been sent to the chemist several times. She, Louisa, was ruthless with the delivered grey powders still, sprinkling them in the minister's food when possible, then sending Purdie up at about four o'clock to see to the study fire, and going up herself in a few moments to sit next door and listen to the steady knocking of the horsehair chaise-longue against the wall; it had happened now several times—well, all that being the case, there was no point in making trouble with Amy herself, who should shortly need the first pillow put in at this rate, for the look of the thing.

Louisa kept the letter—one never knew when to produce it might or might not be advisable—and bestowed it in a drawer. There was of course no question of Amy's writing to any such address, or being informed that it existed.

* * *

Nancy Purdie no longer cleaned the church on Mondays, as Mrs McKitterick had found a man and wife to act as caretakers. However, Nancy did not suffer as regarded money, being well paid for other things. Today, which was early on a Sunday winter's morning, she had been told to come down and keep an eye on the new oil heaters, as if wrongly used they could set the place on fire. Winter was certainly here, and the place would have been freezing without them; as it was, the burners had been lit, were giving out the correct blue flame, and the church by now was pleasantly warm with a nostalgic smell of paraffin, still expensive but less messy than culza, which was all there had been formerly.

While Nancy was bending over the last burner she felt hopeful fingers pinch her bottom. It was, of course, Holy Joe Sproat, unmet with now for some time and no loss; he looked more than ever like a sparrow, his sharp little beak of a nose pinched with the cold outside, his overcoat not yet removed. 'There's time for a quick five meenuts,' he murmured. 'Where ha'e ye been, Nancy? I've missed ye Mondays something fearful.'

She told him he needn't bother, and to keep

his hands to himself. His face turned ugly. 'Some other man, eh?'

'Maybe.' She wasn't going to let him guess about the minister. Nancy had her own feelings about that; a fine strong lover, and although in this life no situation lasted for ever, she liked to make the most of it while it did. Having sent Holy Joe about his business and seen to the wicks of the heaters, she went and sat down in her place in the manse pew; when the party arrived she'd stand up, to show respect. Meantime, she could savour what had happened in general.

She'd rung the bell at once, as they said, that first time of all, with the powdered whisky; but the old bitch didn't know yet. She herself would tell Mrs McKitterick nothing till she had to. Meantime, the church sermons had regained their former hellfire strength; the minister was consoled again, that was it. A man needed comforting. *There, lad, there; that's better, eh?* She would never have thought of herself as talking like that to the minister. By now, he needed her for the time being. What would happen next Nancy left to fate. Young Mrs McPhail had begun to look as if something was happening there as well, but it must have been before he started with herself. Nobody but Solomon—Nancy giggled inwardly—could go on like that with more than one woman at a time.

*   *   *

The congregation entered and soon after that, the manse ladies. It seemed empty in the pew lacking the old widow in her weepers, and altogether there were fewer in church, because of the cold weather everywhere; snow was expected, and no doubt for that reason Sir Phelim Orde and his lady hadn't come today; the journey up by river would be chilly both ways. Nancy sang, with almost as loud a dedication as Louisa herself, when the psalms and paraphrases came to be announced; she'd taken pride in watching the minister ascend to his pulpit, while the beadle shut the stair gate after him. It was flattering to think that this tall dignified man in his black gown and bands was her own valued customer, shaking the horsehair couch like anything.

The sermon began; and Nancy noted a curious thing. Although the Orde pew was empty, anyone would have thought there was somebody sitting there. Mr McPhail kept turning his fine black head towards it, and addressing what was not a bad sermon as if to some absent ghost, his eyes full of fire and at the same time, sadness.

*   *   *

'Purdie, have you been unwell lately?'

She had no business to ask like that, the old

bitch; but the time had come to speak. 'I didn't like to be sure of it, but I think it'll be all right now, Mrs McKitterick,' Nancy replied; no one here would have used anything but an employer's name, not like England where they had to say yes'm. They were back at the manse.

'Well, you may go on working as usual until it cannot be hidden, after which arrangements will be made. You may stop seeing to the study fire in the afternoons.' Euphemisms were too long a word for Nancy; but she did understand that to mean there wouldn't be any more grey powder shaken into the minister's food now and again from a pepper-pot. By this time, he probably didn't need it; he'd got used to having her there, not saying anything, just getting on with it. Well, it was over, at least, provided everything went as planned. Nancy wondered again whether she and Mrs Amy would be neck-and-neck, the minister's wife looked thicker some days than she did others, but some folk were made like that.

CHAPTER FOUR

The intense cold had resolved itself in a flurry of snow, and by night the streets would lie under a thick white blanket. Before that happened, McPhail took himself out to stride grimly up the hill towards Charing Cross, as they called it now; many of the new parts of town had English names. Why Bath Street, up which he was walking? Bath was in Somerset. However, he recalled something about hot and cold baths made available here last century. In any case the naming of streets was the least of McPhail's afflictions, perturbed as his mind was over what he himself was becoming. There was no point in deceiving himself by remembering the Old Testament patriarchs; he himself was a present-day minister, and knew the warnings of St Paul against fornication. He had committed it many times now with Nancy Purdie, and though Nancy herself was without doubt a richly bouncing reward, he should not consider such things, especially as he had seldom even thought of Nancy as an immortal soul, but of the earth earthy. He himself was a married man, and must get a grip on his behaviour; after Amy had had her child, and had recovered, he could resume their permitted state and, perhaps, raise up sons and daughters. The prospect of doing so, even of this coming child, was strange. No doubt, having lacked brothers and sisters of his own age—Jessie had been more like a mother to him—he had lost contact with humanity, and yet had to cater for it by reason of his calling. He must become less unworthy.

To do himself justice, he had for some time been convinced that the pepper Mrs McKitterick had taken to giving him had certain effects. It had a strange flavour, and he recalled the same in Sir Phelim's whisky; maybe there was something of the kind used in the distilling process. He had, at any rate, raised his hand two days ago as his mother-in-law was presiding, as she always did, over the soup tureen at luncheon, ladling out its riches and, in his case, shaking out the pepper straight from a large silver pot into the plate. She wouldn't let Amy have any, saying it was not good for her condition; and didn't take any herself. He had, therefore, said firmly on that occasion, 'No more pepper, pray; I dislike it,' and had taken his soup as it was. It was too soon to say whether or not that was what had been affecting him. An exercise of the will was necessary in any case. In all the years of his manhood he had formerly overcome certain urges. He must become again as he had been before his marriage, at least for the time.

The snow blew in his face, and it would begin to grow dark soon; perhaps they would light the new gas-flares an hour earlier than usual. McPhail blinked the snow from his eyelashes, opened his eyes to behold Brabazon Orde, and all his good intentions vanished on the wind.

She was smiling on her husband's arm, and with the other Sir Phelim was upholding a vast black umbrella for them both against the snow. Brabazon had seen him, McPhail, and they stopped, closer to one another than he remembered ever being; the warmth from her body, swathed in furs, reached him and he no longer felt the cold. He felt no sensation at all, in fact, except astonished joy at her presence; to happen unexpectedly now, this moment, in the street!

He heard his own voice asking them to the manse for shelter and a dram. Sir Phelim smiled, and shook his head.

'We are going down to the carriage-house before it gets dark; we have the river journey to make, as ye know. I have been meaning, minister, to ask you and your good lady to luncheon on a Sunday, after church, when the weather is somewhat better than it is now. The boat will bring ye back, also the carriage at this end, in time for the evening service.'

McPhail said his wife was unable to travel at present. 'Ay, so they say,' agreed Sir Phelim, adding that maybe the voyage by water would after all upset Mrs McPhail. 'Come alone, then; Sproat will be along this week, he and I have matters to discuss. You and this young lady here may entertain one another. She has just been having one of her singing lessons, which I was privileged to hear and witness. Brabazon, ye must sing for the minister when he comes down.'

To hear her sing! He had often noted her strong, sweet voice in church, bringing throbbingly alive Milton's stately old paraphrases. He heard himself accept the invitation for the ensuing Sunday. One must hope the snow would have gone by then, but whether it had or not, he would go. He would go, he told himself, if he had to walk on fire and ice; then told himself not to be a fool. He was in his mid-forties, it was several miles down-river and there were two services to be fitted in and prepared for. He must keep his feet on the ground in all ways. Sir Phelim would send a conveyance, as promised.

* * *

Mrs McKitterick had meantime decided that after all, the presence of Purdie in the house had best be suspended; healthy as Nancy undoubtedly was, continued adventures on the horsehair couch might cause her to miscarry. Louisa therefore arranged for a room to the south of town meantime, with the intention of keeping a firm eye by frequent unheralded visits. Later it would be necessary to bring Purdie within reach of succour. 'Remember,' she told the young woman, 'that if I find evidence of any misbehaviour, your money will stop. On the other hand if everything goes as it should, there will be a substantial reward.' She added that she would give Purdie sewing to do for the missions; it would keep her occupied and out of trouble. Mr McPhail was unlikely to run across her where she was being sent, and if he noticed a lack of Purdie's presence and should venture to ask, Louisa would say she was visiting a sick cousin in Renfrewshire. It was partly true.

Meantime, she had put the first pillow down Amy's front. Asked why—the child was becoming unduly inquisitive—she explained that it was a usual precaution, to make everyone aware of her state. The explanation served as well as any other.

It came to Louisa that, the pillow apart—it was unlikely Mr McPhail would notice its temporary absence at nights—there was now no reason to keep him from visiting Amy or even spending the night with her; in other words, she could have her own room upstairs as she had asked. This was done, and a bed was made up in widow Swords' former quarters, next to the bath Amy seemed to fancy so frequently. However, there was no sound of any nocturnal ascent of the staircase from Mr McPhail, and it seemed evident he had forgotten he was married. No doubt he had other matters on his mind. In any case she herself had done her best, including having written to Uncle Julius to say dear Amy was in an interesting situation, and that he would be sent more precise news as soon as it became available.

*   *   *

The minister kept his feet on the ground that week with difficulty; the days seemed to drag, interminably, until Sunday. He made himself put in the time by carrying out his various duties, visiting the sick folk, going on his occasional parish rounds—these he dreaded, having no small talk, and like all the rest of his calling was unendingly drowned in cups of tea. He also swallowed one more dose of Sproat's milky sugared variety at the lantern-slide hall, and was reminded—as if he needed reminding!—that they would be going down-river together after the next morning service.

'Make it a short sermon, minister,' said Holy Joe, and winked. Aeneas McPhail resented the gesture; it was familiar, and he was accustomed to being treated with respect. However, the man was undoubtedly common. He had been seen lately in the company of the Lord Provost at some Merchants' House meeting, and no doubt had got above himself even more than usual.

The sermon for Sunday was, in fact, about the trumpet that brought down the walls of

Jericho. Whether it was long or short McPhail knew not; he was filled with glory and triumph, seeing Brabazon, still in furs, with her husband, her blue eyes meeting his without pretence or shyness. He was filled with a sense of his own mission. He heard his voice thundering out towards an empty back pew, though the rest of the church was full. Louisa had stayed at home with Amy, who was not feeling at all well; and Purdie was for some reason no longer at the manse. He had forgotten about her in the turmoil of the week. He must remember to ask his mother-in-law what had become of her; servants came and went, however, and already Nancy Purdie seemed like part of another life.

He himself was alive, now, still, today; and after church joined Sproat and Sir Phelim and his wife to walk to the latter's waiting carriage. He had never been certain of the arrangements whereby it was always ready to bring Sir Phelim up from the river; the millionaire explained now, as they drove, what the minister already knew; that it was kept in a stables not far from the manse itself, driven down in time each week by the coachman, who lived with his wife elsewhere, and that Sir Phelim himself now and again used the upstairs living-quarters at the stables as an office; not so often lately, he added, smiling at his wife.

The presence of Brabazon fired McPhail

already, and by the time they boarded the waiting paddle-steamer he could feel the blood beat high in him, as though he had been running. It was chilly on deck, and they all four went downstairs to the saloon, which had padded seats of crimson felt and gave a view of the passing piers and the high grey churning water. Orde and Sproat had begun to talk of business matters; he heard the word rolling-stock, but took little heed of anything but Brabazon herself, seated so that her skirts brushed against him; with the gentle movement of the outward paddles their knees touched without intention. The contact sent tremors through McPhail. He could not remember that they had exchanged a single word; to look was enough, and to touch; coming down the hatchway he had put out his hand to help her, and had felt the grasp of hers. The memory stayed with him.

They docked at Crosslyon jetty, and disembarked, thereafter walking two and two. Out of politeness, Sir Phelim came with the minister, and explained that his wife would maybe have to do the entertaining of him, as he himself had much to discuss with Sproat about the recently uncertain fate of future cotton imports. As such matters were of no interest to McPhail at all, he nodded absently and refrained from comment.

They had reached the gates, where a grey-haired lodgekeeper curtseyed; most of the other servants would be off today, and they themselves would take luncheon ready prepared, as was the Sunday custom. McPhail looked at the famous rose garden, lacking its blossoms for the time and covered with melting snow. By summer it would be magnificent. The winter garden beckoned greenly through its glass, fringed palms pressing against the heated panes. As they walked past, a great sound boomed; the hour, struck on the great clock in the central tower above. Thereafter McPhail was conscious of its heavy tick, tock; that must go on day and night. He expressed interest in the clock. Sir Phelim smiled.

'It means we have arrived on time. I always congratulate the ship's captain if he gets us in before the chime; so far, he has contrived it.'

Tick, tock, tick, tock. They all went in to luncheon.

McPhail never as a rule noticed what he ate, but the food was good today, though mostly cold. The grandeur of the house reminded him that he was a blacksmith's son who had only lately learned to speak of luncheon. He saw Brabazon spoon syllabub delicately into her mouth, always smiling. It was as though their eyes could not help meeting. He was aware of an intense rush of desire.

After luncheon they withdrew to a small alcove, and there was coffee and brandy. The brandy went to McPhail's head; he had not, since the episode of Sir Phelim's whisky-bottle in the manse study, partaken of spirits. He recalled the matter of Purdie at that time, and closed his eyes for instants. Sir Phelim and Sproat were talking on about India, cotton, prospects, an American contract which was about to be renewed or else maybe not. 'I maintain that there will be change coming,' he heard Sproat say.

The clock chimed the new hour. 'My dear,' said Sir Phelim, 'all this talk of business is causing the minister to fall asleep. Take him up and show him the Birmingham clock; the works will interest him.'

She rose; it was as if they had both been waiting for a signal. She preceded him out of the room, her skirts rustling. He was aware of unending corridors of crimson carpeting, then stairs and more stairs, covered likewise. The ticking of the clock grew ever louder. Finally she led him into the clock-chamber, and the sound shut all else out.

It was then they came together. It was inevitable, an almost fluid merging of one being into another; a mingling of two streams of water at last in the sea, making a deep and fathomless current swiftly flowing, further and ever further, into an unknown beyond. He had trembled for a time, and now was still. Tick, tock; tick, tock. Presently, from the world they had left behind, he heard the quarter-chime.

*   *   *

Downstairs, Sir Phelim had heard it also; it was nearly time for the minister to go back, or he would be late for the evening service. Orde dragged his mind away unwillingly from the talk he and Sproat had been having. Sproat had said, and he was a sound man, that although shares would fall shortly because of the current American disputes between north and south, now was the time to buy; it was certainly doubtful that the matter would go as far as civil war, and thereafter whoever owned the bulk of Sea Island cotton would do well.

'I myself am taking a separate gamble, for I have no wife to cater for,' Sproat smiled. 'I am curious to invest in India rolling-stock.'

'Are ye mad, man? The East India Company has been gone a generation, and they left with all they could take, ye may be bound.'

'Nevertheless I think that with the possibilities of native export—mind you, such a matter will be slow—there may be a more varied market than lies in cotton for its own sake. I am a wheen tired of the clattering reels turning, turning, and would be glad to put my own hand to some other thing. I may be as wrong as the next man, but I have my insurance business at my back; whatever comes will not see me in the gutter.'

'I would buy the mill,' said Sir Phelim, as Sproat had been hoping. The old boy couldn't resist the thought of a rise in stocks. By the time the talk was finished, Sproat had sold not only the majority of shares in the Glasgow mill, but others he held in Lancashire. Mentally, he licked his lips. There would be war in the United States, he was privately assured; the North might well blockade the southern ports, thereby delaying bales from reaching the factories for output to the markets. The deficit might not begin to tell this year, as enough was held meantime; next year, however, would be a different thing. As for India, a fortune had been made already out of railways in France; the same thing could happen again with infinitely more profit in so vast a sub-continent, to whoever came first. All of this was for him, Sproat, to explore with the money from the mill sale. He made no change in his expression, though he was calculating the figures already; he could do them in his head.

'I had wanted my wife to sing for ye both,' said Sir Phelim wistfully; thinking, as usual, of Brabazon's future, which would be secure with the ownership of mill shares after his own death, he had not given his mind to all Joe was saying. However, the man was trustworthy, as he knew well. They had done business together for eleven years.

Sproat said now that he would go upstairs and tell the minister to come down. 'He will be taken up with the works,' said Sir Phelim. He himself was immensely proud of the Birmingham clock, and as a rule took everyone personally to see it; but today he was not feeling entirely himself; it must be the effects of the brandy, and he had wanted to talk with Sproat.

Holy Joe vanished, and treading silently, at last ascended the crimson stairs, higher and higher. He deliberately made no sound with his footsteps. When he came to the clock chamber, the loud ticking still drowned all else. They were at it, the two of them, on the floor. The woman was moaning pleasurably He'd suspected as much, the way they'd eyed one another on the way down and earlier. Best to say nothing, know nothing meantime. It was a card to play at some date, without question. The removal from ken of Nancy Purdie nagged at his mind; he would maybe get his own back in some way. He tiptoed out of the clock-chamber entry, down two flights again, then called up, 'Are ye there? It is time for the tide.'

He saw them descend presently, her skirts smoothed, the minister's black clothes brushed free of any dust. The ticking of the great clock followed them, fading slowly but never absent.

'I will leave the pair of ye to see yourselves to the jetty,' said Sir Phelim. 'I'm an old man, and will sleep.'

*　　　*　　　*

Brabazon saw them out; her knees were still weak, and she didn't want to walk down to the jetty beside Sproat. She wanted, now it had happened, to hug it to herself, to be alone. She hoped Sir Phelim wouldn't want to take her to the bedroom today; there was bound to be some sign of what had happened, had so wondrously happened, up there at last beneath the great clock. She would never resent its ticking again; it would remind her, with every stroke, every chime, of now, this day, this past quarter-hour. 'Whenever you want,' she had whispered; and had caressed his rough dark cheek. She was out of the body still, going down in her soul with him, to the waiting boat; he turned once to where she stood at the door, and raised his tall hat, and she lifted her hand, a hostess's polite farewell, no more. Sproat didn't look round. It was as well he'd called out before coming up, otherwise . . . well, that hadn't happened. There must be a next time, and a next. They couldn't separate, now, from one another for long. She might ask Sir Phelim if she could use the coach-house quarters when she went up to town for singing lessons, which she sometimes did alone already with the maid, Phemie; he didn't always come with her. Phemie could be sent shopping. Plans burgeoned in Brabazon's bright brown head; but when she returned to the alcove it was to see Sir Phelim lying on the ground, his balding grey head towards her, and a snoring sound coming from his mouth.

*   *   *

She didn't scream. It was only in books that women screamed when anything went wrong. She knelt down by Sir Phelim and got him into a more comfortable position, kissing him and saying it was all right, she'd send at once for the doctor, who would soon be here; she would run down to the lodge, send word, then come straight back. After that he'd be put to bed. Someone would come. It would only be a few minutes.

'You've been kind to me,' she heard herself whisper. 'You can hear me say it, can you not? I'm going now, at once. They'll come.'

She had seen a tear leave one eye and trickle down his cheek. The cheek looked oddly flat. Half of him seemed all right and the other half not. His good hand groped for hers; he couldn't speak. 'It will not be long,' Brabazon said again; then rose and fled, out of the house, across the garden, down the path. If only the boat hadn't left! But it had; she could see the small shape in the distance, growing smaller. Even if they saw her, it would be too late. The only thing was the lodge: everyone else was away

She knocked on the door; the old woman came. 'You must send for the doctor,'

Brabazon said. 'Sir Phelim is ill. I must get back to him. Please send at once.'

The woman replied that her son in the village would go; the doctor lived a few miles off. 'I will go down, then come up to the house and help ye, my leddy.' They were like that here; reliable and loyal. Brabazon hurried back to Crosslyon, wondering if he would be worse; she'd heard somewhere that seizures were fatal the second time, and this was the first. However, he was lying as she'd left him, and she knelt down again and took him into her arms, as though he'd been a child. They came soon and found them, and carried Sir Phelim upstairs. The doctor said the only thing was for him to rest, and for nothing to trouble or disturb him. A nurse would be sent for. Everything would be arranged.

CHAPTER FIVE

Amy McPhail was not feeling at all well. By now, had Mama but known, the pillow was no longer necessary. It made her heavier than ever, and lately she had had the occasional odd sensation of somebody kicking her from inside. It was gradually becoming clear what being in the family way meant; but she dared ask nothing.

However, on the Sunday in question she was looking so faint and ill that Louisa thought it would be advisable, for many reasons, to indicate to all concerned that the time was drawing near. It was undoubtedly doing so for Nancy Purdie, who had lately been installed in a convenient attic in Nile Street. At the proper time, a little bundle wrapped in a shawl could be conveyed from there under Louisa's mantle quite easily, and installed at the manse.

Today, therefore, the mother and daughter did not attend church. Amy was told to go and lie down; after all, she had demanded the use of a room to herself. 'Luncheon will be sent up on a tray.' Mrs McKitterick stated. That, later on, would impress the minister, who otherwise seemed increasingly absent-minded nowadays. No doubt he was missing Nancy.

Louisa moved about downstairs seeing to the arrangement of the dishes; the table for luncheon had been laid last night as usual before the parlour-maid went off. Once that had been done she felt it her duty to look in again on Amy. She went upstairs to find Amy lying in bed with her brow covered with sweat in large, cold beads. The child must be really ill.

A shocking thing happened then. Louisa had put her hand out to feel the girl's forehead, and Amy shrank away. 'Go away,' she breathed. 'Don't touch me.'

She must be delirious; had there been something odd lately in the food? She wasn't feverish, and yet in her right mind would never have said such a thing. Louisa hesitated, uncertain for once how to act; then the matter was resolved for her. From underneath the covers came the unmistakable sound of a muffled cry. Louisa whipped them off. There, in a mess of wetness and some blood, lay a small baby boy with red hair. His likeness to the departed Highland coachman was unmistakeable.

*　　*　　*

There are moments in life when one acts without thinking. Louisa could not afterwards remember how she got Amy seen to, rolled off the soaking side of the bed on to the dry one, the cord cut—it must have been with her own nail-scissors—and the child wrapped quickly in a pillow-case after wiping its nose and mouth. Nobody had told Louisa how to do anything of the kind, and a deep knowledge must have come either from inheritance, or else suppressed memory of what had been done to herself at Amy's birth. She found herself massaging the girl's flaccid body, disposing of what must be got rid of; then looked round for something with which to keep Amy warm; the blankets were sodden.

Hunting desperately—Mrs Swords hadn't left much behind—she opened a cupboard, and there hung salvation; the abandoned black overcoat of the late Dr Swords, not having been given to the poor for some reason. It had other uses now. Louisa wrapped Amy in it, told her to lie still and on no account to try to do anything at all till she, her mother, came back; then caught up the baby in its wrapping, hurried out of the room, and put on her bonnet and cloak in the hall. Mercifully there were no servants here today, everyone being at church somewhere or other; she hoped Purdie wasn't. In any case she had the key to the Nile Street rooms. It was not far to walk.

Amy, having suppressed long agony, lay exhausted in the heavy ministerial overcoat. At least it was dry; she'd begun to shiver. It smelt of dust. She hadn't even seen the baby.

*　　*　　*

Purdie was in, because her condition by now made it inadvisable to go out. Mrs McKitterick called upstairs daily with milk and food, and had suggested that she, Nancy, stop sewing for the missions and begin making a child's garments instead. It needn't have taken the old bitch to suggest it, Nancy thought; who did she think she was? However, she paid for cloth and wool, and Nancy knitted little vests and sewed diapers to pass the time. Whatever else was to happen to this coming baby it wouldn't be left naked. She had begun to be quite fond of it, feeling it grow in her till by now, she told herself, she couldn't see her own feet. She was eating well, and assured herself she felt fine. The old bitch—it was going to be difficult to call Mrs McK., anything else—had promised money, but she, Nancy, now thought she'd ask for her place back at the manse as well. She had some right, after all, to see what was being done to her own child. As for Mrs Amy's, there hadn't been any word.

The door opened and the old bitch entered, carrying something inside her cloak. She handed the bundle grimly to Nancy, who laid it in her lap in silence. 'I will have to leave him here with you till other arrangements can be made,' Louisa said. 'You must water the milk two-thirds, and feed him with a clean cloth soaked at the corners. When your own child is born they can share your milk.' She would not have talked in this way to a woman of her class; working girls needed to be told very little, however.

Purdie guessed the situation at once, lifting away the pillow-case to glimpse the red head. There was no doubt whom it looked like; so that had been going on, eh? These soft-spoken Highlanders were worse than anybody. Who would have thought Mrs Amy had the spirit for it? Did the minister suspect anything? Probably not; and it was best to say nothing now or later. Nancy did say, however, that if she was to do all that and keep quiet, she'd expect her place at the manse again when it was all over, as well as the money.

Louisa McKitterick rolled up her eyes, and agreed. Events were overtaking her; she wasn't even sure whether or not to inform Uncle Julius that a boy had been born. It was no doubt best to wait for the second birth before deciding one way or the other.

* * *

The news of Sir Phelim Orde's illness reached the manse, and McPhail made haste to go down, without any motive but to console the sick man. He would travel by public steamer. He left, accordingly, early in the week, telling his mother-in-law not to expect him back till night. This suited Louisa, as it was time to visit Purdie on what might, from her own calculations, be a special day, though it was of course not certain. What was so was that Amy seemed feverish, with two bright spots of colour in her cheeks; by now, though, she'd been washed and put between fresh sheets and dry blankets. Nothing had been said; it was the best way; only a single word of warning or else reproach had passed Louisa's lips despite herself. 'Never trust any man's promises,' she told her daughter. 'You have seen for yourself, what can happen.' Amy did not know, of course, that she herself had seen that letter. No doubt the fellow had deluded her with hopes of some kind; least said, soonest mended.

After she had gone Amy lay still for the time, though soon she would begin tossing in high fever; had anyone known, old Dr Swords had been a noted visitor to the Infirmary fever-wards in that same coat. Meantime, Amy's mind remained clear; slow tears welled in her eyes and began to course slowly down her cheeks once her mother had gone. Whatever had happened, Seumas would have let her know by now if he'd meant to write. *It will perhaps be a little while.* It was nine months. Enough money could have been made in that time. He'd forgotten her; and she didn't want to go on living. She'd once asked Mama about the baby, and was told certain things had to be seen to, and not to trouble herself, as Mama knew best what to do. In any case Amy had no milk.

*   *   *

Mr McPhail stood on the deck during the voyage, with the boat crowded; families were going down-river early for the spring holiday. He would get off at Row—his MacGregor blood still led him to think of it as Rhu, but everything had to be English now—and walk back from the public jetty there to Crosslyon. He disembarked with others, and found to his distaste that a presence was walking beside him; Mr Sproat, with a portfolio under his arm and a rolled umbrella in case it rained. McPhail had forgotten his own.

'A good day to ye, minister,' said the man, whom McPhail disliked more than ever without knowing why; certainly it was understandable that he should be here today, he had shared business interests with poor Sir Phelim. 'I trust the patient is well enough to be able to discuss a few matters, but if not it will have done no harm to visit him,' remarked the session-clerk. 'You yourself must go in first, however; the comfort of religion is a great thing.' He leered in an inexplicable way, and McPhail disliked him yet the more.

They were admitted, and the maid, on enquiry, said Sir Phelim was better than he had been; her young ladyship had sat up all night with him, and he'd taken broth from a spouted cup. The doctor had called, and said he'd be back, but not urgently; the thing required was rest. Having ascertained as much, they went up to the sickroom. Brabazon rose, seeming as usual; for a young woman who'd been up all night she looked fresh and not jaded. Sir Phelim was propped up by pillows, his face lopsided. 'My husband can use only his left hand meantime,' Brabazon told the men. 'He is glad you have come.'

She stayed by the window while McPhail had a few words with the patient, then came out with the minister when Sproat went in, the latter having waited meantime on the outer landing. 'You will not tire him,' Brabazon said, having taken on a certain authority. It was shed as soon as Sproat had gone. The pair, left to themselves, held hands, like children. Presently she spoke.

'It would not be right for us here, while he is ill,' she said. 'It was good of you to come. Hold my hand till Mr Sproat comes out. Let us go down to the winter garden; it's private there, and I've been sitting for long.'

They went downstairs to where the green fringed palms and other exotic plants grew rampant inside their glass protection. Brabazon ran her fingers among the fronds; there was a camellia nearby, and its smooth whiteness made him compare it to her flesh. Holding her hand was like holding a flower, except that he could feel the hot blood beating, beating, desirous as his own. Like her, he knew it would be wrong to make love while the sick man lay upstairs. It was always wrong, according to God's law he sought to obey; yet she was so near, so near!

'Listen quickly,' Brabazon said. 'I asked my husband about this earlier; he can still hear me and try to speak. I am to use his little office above the coach-house on Saturdays, and stay over for church. I will have to bring Phemie with me, but she can go to the shops. If you will come to me there in the afternoon, we can be alone for a time.' It would be assumed she had gone for lessons to Madame Padovani's; she knew it was deceitful but could not help it; no more, she knew, could he.

'I will come,' he promised. Presently they heard Sproat walk downstairs. The ticking of the clock sounded faintly beyond, muffled by the shut greenhouse door.

Sproat had made sure of Sir Phelim. As before, he assured him that the rumoured outbreak of war in the United States was unlikely, that the quota of Sea Island cotton should be signed for by contract, in fact increased from last year. 'Other folk may hesitate, and you will be in a most favourable position. I myself am putting what remains to me into shares for the mill.' In plain fact he had invested in Deccan cotton, saying nothing; also a certain amount in wool and Irish flax, to tide things over at the mill itself; he still managed it.

Sir Phelim's good eye slewed round. He was

feeling too tired to decide anything, knew he had not long usefully to live, and was anxious to provide for Brabazon. Good Joe Sproat had after all advised him in time to avoid the collapse of the Western Bank some years ago. He would be a safe trustee.

* * *

Holy Joe had brought pens and paper, the last already made out by mutual agreement with Sir Phelim's lawyers. The draft put him, Joseph Sproat, in charge of all financial matters under trust; unsold property, the distillery, the mills here and in Lancashire, the rest.

He proffered the pen. Sir Phelim signed, with his good remaining hand, the order that would bankrupt his widow.

PART II

CHAPTER ONE

'I should like,' said the Lord Provost dreamily, 'to see a water-closet installed in every house in the city of Glasgow. Now that Her Gracious Majesty has turned on the Loch Katrine supply it should not be an impractical notion.'

Bailie Sproat, newly elected to that honour, looked down his nose. He had been one of the few present to miss making his bow, the Queen's visit having taken place more than two years ago now, to much preparation and the drift of October leaves nearby the magic glitter of the acquired Perthshire loch. He himself had not, at that time, been even a councillor, and had had to wait till November, the customary month for elections, when one endured vulgar hecklings from all and sundry and, in the end and by greasing of certain palms, had succeeded.

He was in the huff, therefore, both because of that and because it seemed impossible to get away from the Reverend Aeneas McPhail, whose turn it had been today to open the council meeting with the accustomed prayer. It was true that the Kirk no longer had the powers it once had, for instance to condemn scolding women to the pillory on such occasions, but even being in a small room with a man of the size and presence of McPhail was like encountering Ben Cruachan. Sproat felt himself reduced in size and importance accordingly, which should not have been allowed.

He turned his thoughts, while the Provost droned on, to the matter of the Loch Katrine supply, which seemed sensible on the face of it but which had encountered tremendous difficulties, not connected with engineering—that had been simple—but with vested interests. There had been the folk who owned shares in the Gorbals water supply, familiar but long known to be impure; the others who had put their money on Loch Lubnaig, further away and darker in colour owing to natural deposits; and not least the man who, when everything was almost settled, had announced in the papers that too pure a source meant that the lead in the pipes would dissolve easily and poison everyone who drank.

That had been by no means all. The slumbering thoughts of my Lords of the Admiralty had been awakened in London by the controversy in the papers, and had produced one of their fiats, which were notoriously difficult to reverse, especially since that other antique body, the House of Lords, saw fit to back them up. It was feared, by some illustrious old salt or other, that the drawing off of fresh water for use by the citizens of Glasgow would lead to a diminution of power in the waters of the Forth, into which those of

Loch Katrine eventually drained, and would cause delay in naval tactics. That hurdle had finally been overcome, and by now the City Council was able to regard the matter as of academic interest and to concentrate on the supply of clothing, blankets and coals to those suffering from the recent loss of employment over the cotton disaster. It was true that they were less severely affected here than in places like Blackburn, but it was still necessary to help the afflicted folk and their families or else, as last century, to assist them with passages to Canada or else to Queensland.

Sproat listened with half an ear; he was well out of danger as regarded financial loss, which had hit unwary folk like Sir Phelim Orde and countless others. Many insurance businesses were in ruin, and he had been careful to underplay the state of his own and, partly, to have himself insured elsewhere. By now he, Joseph Sproat, was a warm man, a respected bailie of the City of Glasgow, in a position to have a say in the running of everything from markets to jails. As regarded markets, it was a pity the meeting had had to be convened on the appointed twice-weekly day of the municipal dog and bird market, just outside in the Candleriggs; twitterings, barkings and yelpings had disturbed the sonority of McPhail's opening prayer and by now almost drowned those of the speaking members who suffered from any kind of hesitancy or lack of address.

Holy Joe, aware that his own pending words would fail to carry their due significance, became in a worse temper than before. However, he reflected that, after all, he had his own private revenge, if not on the dogs and canaries at least on McPhail. The trouble was that nobody must know if he was to preserve his civic reputation. To boast was inadvisable, if tempting.

He heard the Dean of Guild rustle papers; the man should by rights not be present at all. However, it had become customary to admit him, although the City Hall itself, by now twenty-odd years built, was already, like the previous four or five, growing too small for their requirements. It had been happening since the days of the first and second Tolbooth, and but for the depression everywhere there would be plans submitted for the building of a final grand Municipal Building to last for all time. As it was, it would have been better to hold this meeting on the day of the cheese market, which was quiet and for once, unsupervised by the city authorities. Sproat resolved to make his view on this and other matters known in proper course.

* * *

McPhail himself had noticed the crowd outside on the excellently paved street. Many were in a bad way. It was not permitted, within the royalty of the burgh, to sell for gain unless licensed, which meant that the playing of bagpipes for pence or the selling of toffee apples to relieve necessity was forbidden. It was almost like the days when licensed beggars wore brass badges; there was nothing for the ruined folk to do but stand and stare. Like everywhere else this year the list of insolvencies was longer than anywhere in living memory; the good ladies of Oakdale Church had been foremost in giving aid to the unfortunate, though Sir Phelim Orde, ruined himself, could not join in, nor his lady.

McPhail saw them standing now, the folk who had lost all they had, or, like his own ancestors after the Clearances in the north, had nothing left to lose. Then, they had come south to find work, and many had prospered; now, prosperity was less easy in the state of the present American civil war and its aftermath, striking at them here across the Atlantic. McPhail saw the detritus washed up by the tide of the late depression; barefoot keelies, veterans from the Crimea lacking an arm or eye or leg; indigent persons, bankrupt insurance brokers, drunkards going blind with Red Biddy, former jailbirds, folk from the Saltmarket who had ventured meantime out of what was almost a ghetto where the police dared not go. Behind all of it, the dogs and caged birds and puppies for sale yelped and barked and twittered; he heard them not with irritation like Sproat, but with sadness; many of the puppies would be cruelly abandoned once their purchasers had grown tired of them. Stray dogs grew up, bred, and would not conform to legislation, arousing certain sympathy in McPhail.

He made this the substance of his prayer, reminding the council that man had from the beginning misused the gifts of God. He dwelt on the fact that Glasgow had once been a place of pure springs and wells, where the patron saint, St Mungo, had chosen to make his abode by the Molendinar Burn because of its health-giving properties. Since then, the source had been fouled up by the habits of man; and no doubt the essence of his prayer had given rise to the Lord Provost's untoward remark about water-closets. The sanitary and infectious state of the city, McPhail had said, was an example of the way man misused God's gifts. He had prayed at some length that the city council, now in session with their well-fed faces turned towards himself, might see a way to avert such evils in the future as had occurred in the past; following on which the Lord Provost had made his hopeful statement.

* * *

Having a soul above such things in general, McPhail stopped listening to the council's deliberations and returned to thoughts of the saint. It was said St Mungo—his real name was Kentigern—had stood each night in all weathers in the Molendinar until he had recited the entire Psalter, but this was no doubt an accretion over the centuries; the good man would have caught his death instead of living, as was also rumoured, to the age of one hundred and eighty-seven years. One psalm each night was more reasonable, and royal Columba had visited Mungo when the latter's hair was white, and there had been great joy at their meeting.

McPhail had in fact discovered a number of facts about the life of St Mungo while he was a divinity student; he was interested in such things and in the separation of truth from myth. The accepted version of events was that St Mungo had been a virgin birth to a votaress named Thenew, who had herself later on had a burn named after her which ran into the Clyde, the Glaswegians having modified her name to Enoch. The new City and Union Railway had greatly interfered with the burn, and even the Molendinar was by now little more than a sewer, ending also in the Clyde; not, these days, a savoury end.

McPhail reflected on what he had read from the old Celtic sources. Thenew herself had been a princess, the daughter of King Loth, after whom Lothian had been named. By an earlier marriage he had produced Mordred, who in the end had brought about the death of King Arthur. McPhail recalled seeing the great bulk of Arthur's Seat rearing beyond Holyrood on a visit he had made to the General Assembly with Amy and, of course, her mother. There was no doubt Arthur had been in these parts; and the princess Thenew had shared his Christian faith in those early times. She had wanted to dedicate her life to God, but King Loth had decided that she marry a young prince named Ewain, son of a local king. On her continued refusal, Loth had most uncharitably given her in charge of a swineherd. The tale went that while in this humble situation, the rejected prince had discovered her and, once more refused, had ravished her. Thenew, found thereafter to be pregnant, was mocked at for forsaking her vows and was cast by her father and others over Traprain Law. Having great faith she prayed on the way down and landed safely, whereupon the enraged king put her in a coracle and cast her on the stormy waters of the Forth. McPhail wondered if the legend of Danaë, to whom much the same thing had happened, had caused confusion here. By whatever means, Thenew survived once again, landed at Culross and there found a fire of cold ashes. It lit itself miraculously and, warm at last, she gave birth safely to a son. Meantime, the swineherd had killed King Loth with a dagger, which made McPhail wonder if perhaps there was some personal involvement in that quarter, but nobody seemed to have thought of it.

Swineherd's son or prince's, the boy was handed over by his mother, who desired to continue as a votaress, to an old hermit named Servanus, who exclaimed at sight of the child, 'You are my dear one! You are my dear one!'

Love was like that; instant, undying. *You are my dear one, Brabazon.* He returned prudently to thoughts of saints.

Servanus' other followers had become jealous of the dear one, had killed the old man's pet robin and blamed Kentigern, who restored it to life. The same thing happened with a fire he was ordered to tend; they put it out, and he lit it once more with a green bough. The bird and the bough, with other emblems, were shown now on the city's coat of arms at the end of the Lord Provost's chain of office; McPhail stared at it as the meeting proceeded. A bird, a tree, a bell, a fish. The fish had been a salmon caught by an unfaithful queen on Mungo's instructions, having been told that she would find a gold ring in its mouth, given by her once to a lover and found and cast into the water by her husband the king. *Go and catch a fish, Simon, and you will find a coin in its mouth to pay the temple tax for both of us.* That text was not often enough preached, being considered frivolous. The king and queen had been reconciled and she had thereafter continued faithful. Now, on the coat of arms, more was remembered than they knew of today.

The tree that never grew,
The bird that never flew,
The fish that never swam,
The bell that never rang,
Let Glasgow flourish by the preaching of the Word.

Well, he was doing his best with that last at any rate; and the meeting seemed now to be discussing the Clyde, which was far from a state these days to support salmon or any other fish; it stank in summer and at low tide, when the effluent poured into it became manifest to the nostrils. McPhail heard Sproat put his oar in.

'Certain proportions of lime and ammonium sulphate could be condensed at a point forth of the city, and piping led directly thence from the sewers, with great benefit.'

No doubt the likes of Sproat would see that something was done about everything. McPhail's thoughts returned to St Mungo, who had at last parted from Servanus and journeyed westward, over rough paths, with the body of a holy man, Fergus, in a cart which was drawn by two untamed bulls.

The colt of a foal no man has yet ridden. He might make a sermon of such things, untamed and untouched till they were needed to show the power of God. Samson, strong till his hair was cut; the long-haired Frankish Merovings, discredited now as *rois fainéants* but powerful in their cures, so that the church, having anointed a successor, had tonsured the last of them and forced him into a monastery. It was however not advisable to regale the elders of the kirk with too much truth from the past. Sproat remained one of these, as it was prestigious.

St Mungo had, at any rate, buried Fergus near the Molendinar; there was a carving in the cathedral with the name and a picture of the cart, and St Mungo's tomb itself had somehow escaped the Reformation and was still in the crypt. He remembered standing over it when he had passed his final examinations, staring down at the plain dark stone.

The meeting was over, evidently; he had hardly heard a word of it. He would return by way of the noisy market past where, not so long ago, an enterprising dairy farmer had kept three hundred cows and had sold water piped from elsewhere at a halfpenny a stoup, and had died a rich man. Water was needed for life.

* * *

Outside, as Sproat emerged in civic dignity

later on, two women began yelling from the crowd. They had once been among the bandy-legged lasses from his mill, had lost their jobs and had found work instead in the fish market, which closed early. He walked straight past, giving no sign that he had heard or that he knew such persons. They avenged themselves.

'See yon wee spurgie wha went ben, and now he's out, cockie-breekie, wi' a chine roun his shouthers, thinkin' he's God Himsel'?'

'I'd string him up wi't.'

'I'd hing a haddie's guts roun' his wame. He'd ken fine what to dae then.'

The crowd tittered, to the temporary relief of its depression. Sproat gave no indication of how mortified he felt. Unfortunately, the erstwhile powers of a bailie to bring malefactors to court for breach of the peace were going the same way as the kirk's vanished powers to pillory scolding women. All such benefits—and Sproat would have liked to use them now—were to be made over shortly to the Police Commission: a pity.

However, he thought he had made his mark about the sewage. Like McPhail, and as the only similarity in the two men's thinking, Sproat was aware that there had once been salmon caught in the Clyde. He kept his nose in the air, and walked past the jeering crowd and the noise of dogs, canaries and parrots, thinking constructively of how he could make his mark on the next scheduled meeting. If the

Provost wanted his water-closets, the resultant flow might make it advisable to join Loch Arklet to Loch Katrine by cast-iron pipes. He would suggest it.

CHAPTER TWO

Some weeks thereafter, the bailies were scaling. The term was no longer used for anybody else. However, watching the chosen fourteen emerge in their historic grandeur of cocked hats, chains of office, furs and civic insignia, the fish that never swam, the bell that never rang and all the rest of it, McPhail, watching, reflected that no matter whether you spelt the word scale or skail it had once meant several things; to come out of a meeting, as here; to fire a gun, to jut outwards, to give up housekeeping—he smiled—and it could mean a thin, shallow vessel for skimming milk, or else the noise of waves breaking on the shore. The Scots vernacular was rich in its economy, but had become unfashionable in the best circles, like Oakdale.

As regarded that, the newly elected Bailie Sproat was among them, his rodent's visage suitably grave and as pompous as a rat could be. McPhail was still uncertain why he so disliked the man, but the dislike had increased since Sproat had unctuously donated the largest sum of any to provide an annuity for Brabazon Orde following her husband's recent bankruptcy The old Sir Phelim lingered on, but after a third stroke no longer had all his wits outwardly. Whether or not he realised that he had lost everything was doubtful; certainly all items of value in Crosslyon had been sold off, and an undisclosed buyer found whom McPhail suspected, without evidence, to be Holy Joe. The latter had achieved his heart's dream of the grand civic position last year, after, from all outward appearance, losing money like other folk owing to the American civil war. Although stocks of cotton had not been in immediate danger, the year following there had been a famine lacking any, as the North had blockaded the southern ports as forseen, to prevent export. Sproat had accepted his losses with becoming humility outwardly, but still appeared able to finance what he chose.

McPhail himself was not sorry Brabazon was no longer rich; it brought her nearer to him. It had been he who suggested to the session of elders that, as Sir Phelim had been a most generous founder of Oakdale church in his day, they should do something for his young wife, who was penniless. Sproat had come forward, as stated. It was unpleasant to think of Brabazon's owing him gratitude; they hadn't discussed it together. It was a sensitive point, as McPhail himself had only his stipend and had been able to do relatively little.

Crosslyon was a sad place to visit now, with the concrete cracking on the neglected garden paths, and the great clock ticking away the hours and years above the empty, echoing rooms and corridors. It had proved impossible to remove the clock without destroying it. No doubt the sick man heard it still from where he lay, nursed by three women; Brabazon herself, Phemie the maid, and old Mrs Mackay from the lodge, who had stayed on without payment. They would take one another's place as the days and nights passed, one sitting with the patient and the other two left meantime free.

He would see her, therefore, tomorrow, in the little upstairs house in the lane, where no carriage waited now in the empty space below. Permission had been given for Lady Orde to make use of the rooms when she came to town; whoever might have purchased the Orde estate did not require them meantime. McPhail passed by the house now, striding uphill after the session meeting which had taken him into town in the first place. He did not glance at the windows, which sparkled. Phemie, good soul, kept the place neat and clean, and laid in food for when Brabazon came up by the public steamboat. He himself would go to her tomorrow, treading on air all the way Today, however, he must put in an appearance at the manse with his family, as it was known; he lifted an eyebrow. There was the little dark-haired daughter Amy had borne him, who resembled him in colouring; Purdie's boy, however, had red hair. McPhail frowned, feeling his sense of the proprieties return with a slap. Nobody could be the father but that departed coachman, and it offended him that Purdie should have been entertaining the pair of them at once; he preferred to forget the matter, as there was nothing else to be done. Amy's severe attack of scarlet fever, from which she had never fully recovered after their daughter's birth, had occupied the minister's awareness to the exclusion of the fact that Purdie's morals were not all they might be and that he ought to speak to her about it.

Nevertheless it was inadvisable to send Purdie packing, and he did not genuinely want to; oddly, his mother-in-law defended her, saying she was a good worker and should stay, and be allowed to keep the little boy with her. McPhail was uncertain exactly when the three, including his own baby daughter who had been left with her at nurse, had returned; it must have been after the full-scale stripping and whitewashing necessary upstairs after Amy's scarlet fever, when a great deal had had to be got rid of and burned. One must trust that, by now, the infection did not linger. Amy, by reason of all of it, slept downstairs again with her mother, and McPhail hardly saw her or thought of her as other than Louisa's shadow. He himself lived from one Saturday to the next; the rest of the week was filled in with duties which had become of increasingly less interest and importance. He had begun to dislike the parish visiting; it seemed to consist of unending calls on prosperous folk who were pleased with themselves and needed no counsel. McPhail thought of Christ and the Pharisees; there was maybe an analogy there. At least he'd lost Sproat as the session-clerk, with his grand appointment now; the man had no time, and they had not yet found another to fill the post permanently.

He came to the manse, ascended the steps past the carriage-block, which the maids kept whitened twice weekly. The carriage itself was mostly used on Sundays, to take Louisa, himself and Purdie and the two children down to Oakdale. Lately they had taken to calling in for Brabazon as well; it had been Louisa's suggestion. Lady Orde mustn't lose touch now her husband was unable to come, as she was in town in any case. It made an odd assortment in the carriage, with nobody knowing the whole truth except himself.

*　　　*　　　*

Next day, he sat gloriously naked at a table in the coach-house quarters, writing his sermon; he'd brought the rough notes with him as usual. It was summer, and the room was full of sunlight from the small window-panes Phemie kept shining and clean despite the buzzing flies. She, or someone—he hadn't asked—had put a pot of bright geraniums on the inside sill. He stared at them, then turned once more to the woman on the bed, laying down his pen. Naked also, she was Eve to his Adam; *the rose of Sharon, the lily of the valley. O thou whom my soul loveth, O thou fairest among women; open to me, my love, my dove, my undefiled; I am my beloved's and my beloved is mine; he feedeth among the lilies.*

They lay together yet again; and Brabazon's white fingers played with the handsomest side-whiskers in Glasgow. This, she thought, must be like Eden before the Fall; it wasn't true what Milton said, they'd studied *Paradise Lost* at Mrs McIntyre's, or tried to. Without this, it wouldn't have been paradise. After all they'd been able to watch the animals doing the same thing and were bound to think of it for themselves, much earlier.

The pomegranates budded . . . or ever I was aware, my soul made me like the chariots of Amminadib.

His preaching, he knew, was different. Brabazon's body and soul inspired gentleness, the love of God rather than God's wrath. She was his beloved child as well as his mistress; *how beautiful are thy feet with shoes, O prince's daughter!* Yet she was more beautiful still with none, even her little toes with nails like sea-shells. *The joints of thy thighs are like jewels, thy belly a round goblet.* He caressed it, and went later to finish the phrases of his sermon before he dressed. Outside, the sun shone in past the bright geraniums, and it was quiet in the lane.

*   *   *

Her blue eyes watched him with devotion and a kind of sadness. If he noticed the last, he assumed it to be because of her sick old husband, of whom she was fond. He again told himself their loving did Sir Phelim no harm.

*   *   *

It was possible; she had once murmured, that he guessed it; he had never, in the days when he could still speak, asked questions about where she went, what she did on Saturdays. It was true that the public steamboat didn't run on the Sabbath, and if she wanted to come up to town it was necessary to leave on the day before.

He kissed her for the last time, dressed, and left, putting his tall hat on his head as he emerged downstairs into the lane. She had flung on a bedgown to see him out, and stood for instants behind the door, hair hanging loose. Her expression was no longer serene; she was thinking of what must happen tomorrow, after church was over and they had left her here alone.

*   *   *

The journey to church proceeded as usual.

The carriage drew up outside next morning, with the ladies of the manse, Nancy Purdie in charge of the two children, and McPhail himself silent, intent on the reins; they did not now employ a coachman. Arriving, the main party entered the pew; the church was already partly full. Louisa nodded to acquaintances in the Sewing Circle, seated here and there. Amy stared ahead of her. She looked like an old woman since the birth and the subsequent illness; it was not expected of her to take part in anything. She stood and sat with the rest during the service, thinking her own bitter thoughts.

The sight of the little red-haired boy beside Purdie reminded her of Seumas' perfidy. Not only had he never written, but must have been having an affair with Purdie at the same time as—as that single encounter, unforgotten; the only time in all her life that she had lived. Well, it was over, and no doubt she should be fonder of her little daughter, who greatly resembled, of course, Mr McPhail. The two children were well drilled and well behaved, and sat quietly in the pew.

Louisa herself, looking along the row, felt triumph. She had managed the whole thing discreetly, and if anyone now asked the identity of the red-haired boy it was easy to turn the enquiry aside as one would do for any indiscretion of a servant. Purdie could take the blame, and had already done so equably even in the face of open disapproval and stares from certain ladies who sat forever in judgment.

The only thing that troubled Louisa faintly was the memory of a letter from Uncle Julius, some time after the switched births. *Ahur tells me, with his especial sight, that a boy has been born to Amy. Why have you not written? Is he deformed? Send information.* She had done so; saying the little boy was well, but she had not had leisure to write earlier because of poor Amy's fever, which had taken a long time to mend, and there had been all the stripping and whitewashing later on to render the rooms free of infection. She hoped he was well, and promised to bring little Eddie to see him when he was older. He had been christened Edward. Louisa had no idea why she had chosen the name, except that it was as different as possible from James. There must be no reminder of that unfortunate business with the now departed coachman. Amy had, without doubt, repented of her ways, and after all had the consolation of Purdie's little girl, who resembled Amy's husband. It had all worked out conveniently; except that the red hair was difficult to explain. The faculty of Ahur for seeing what other folk didn't had evidently raised doubts about the boy Edward's legitimacy. She only hoped neither he nor Uncle Julius would encounter anybody from Oakdale.

The service concluded—Louisa realised she

had not heard a word of the sermon—they drove back, Lady Orde declining an invitation to luncheon. She had, she said, an appointment in the early afternoon with Mrs McIntyre, who always invited her to Sunday tea.

*   *   *

Brabazon herself had been unable to eat much of the food Phemie had left provided. She poured a little milk from the covered jug, knowing it wouldn't keep fresh as long as tomorrow. Afterwards she put on her bonnet again, and a veil; then waited. At the precise accustomed time, a closed carriage drew up outside; she went down, locking the upper house door, and was helped in by Sproat's coachman. The bailie himself had not come; he was careful not to be seen in the wrong places. Brabazon clenched her gloved hands in her lap as they drove through the silent Sabbath streets; one or two couples were already out walking, the wives doucely on their husbands' arms. Their own wheels made the only sound, and they drove some way out of town.

At first, when she had been brought this way, it had been unfamiliar; she had not known where she was being taken until the sight of the mills, and the ginning sheds, told her.

There would be nobody about, of course, today; although since the failure of the cotton *he'd* taken to wool-spinning and some linen from Irish flax. However, the profits, if any, would be his own.

She grimaced bitterly. He had put the state of affairs to her, one day down at Crosslyon, walking with her up and down the deserted paths with their overgrown lawns; there was no longer a gardener employed. She had been saddened to have to see the place go downhill, and it must have shown in her face; Sproat, who had been upstairs to see Sir Phelim, fingered her upper arm possessively, and said, 'Ay. It's not what it once was. However, at least Sir Phelim has a roof over his head, and is not put out on the streets, as might have happened. Ye have myself to thank for that, and other things.'

She had wondered what the things were; auditors had settled the estate, selling off the paddle-steamer to the city of Glasgow, taking away for sale every item in the house which was of value, except her harp. That had been her own property, and they'd left it. At times Sir Phelim, struggling to speak, would ask her to play. Now—

'It is time to pay me for maintenance, Brab, and your man's. I have waited awhile.' She saw his small eyes survey her, with an expression she disliked. She drew away from his touch.

'I do not like to be called that,' she said, and

turned her head to watch the drifting leaves on the path; it was October again, and they would soon lie thick like leaves in Vallombrosa. She heard his smug laugh.

'I can call ye by any name I choose, my lass, for I own the pair of ye, and the minister forbye. He comes to ye on a Saturday, eh? Did ye suppose naebody keened? I will have ye on a Sunday; that suits all of us. They would, most certainly, discharge him were it known he has criminous intercourse wi' another man's wife on any day at all. He also would be out on the streets, and his family; and what else can he da'e but preach the gospel? Maybe he'd take to a gipsy's cart, and go round the countryside with them all, eh? It wouldna be a safe living, like he has now. No, I will not come to the coach-house, though I own it with the rest. I will send the carriage, and ye will come to me where I direct, and will thereafter do as ye are bid.'

That had been the essence of it; and what choice had she? Two helpless men—and McPhail in such ways was as helpless as Sir Phelim—would pay the penalty if she did not, as Sproat put it, do as she was bid.

She had toed the line in such ways for some time now, and was being driven for it to happen again. The mills came in sight, and Brabazon set her lips firmly and made ready to descend. She knew where his office was, past the looming empty machines, across a floor which echoed to her footsteps. The carriage would wait to escort her back, later.

*   *   *

It was an hour and a half before she returned; this time, he'd shown her himself to the factory door. 'Next week again, eh?' It had become habit; always the same, with his greeting her unseen by anyone, his small mouth and stubby hands avid, but containing himself and, after reaching the inner room, throwing himself idly down in the armchair, eyeing her.

'Undress.' And he'd watch her. The very way he sat by custom was an insult; so was what followed when she was ready, and had lain down on the bed. She was used by now to his cock-sparrow thrustings, and as usual turned her head aside in disdain; suddenly, she heard his voice rasping, felt the hands squeeze and pinch angrily

'Warm tae't, lass, or I'll skelp your bum. Jump tae't, ye bitch, ye.'

It was intolerable, but she had to pretend that she minded less than she did. She must endure whatever he chose to do, even the groping and clutching of his mean, precise grasp all over her. The hands were short-fingered, a clerk's who had begun by adding up numbers. His legs were short as well, and had wound by now about her own. He was a swine; she could hear his gruntings. It didn't matter;

there was a place he would never reach. *My beloved is white and red, and chief among ten thousand. His locks are bushy, and black as a raven.* Brabazon kept her eyes shut.

'Ye'll be gaun tae the evening service now, eh?' He snickered, satisfied.

She did not reply. After it was over she dressed again wordlessly, drew down her veil and left. She hoped the coachman didn't know who she was. When they reached the little house again she went inside, heated water and washed herself all over. Even then she didn't feel clean. If Phemie had been here these days, she would have had hot water ready; but Phemie was with Sir Phelim. She herself didn't need a maid any more.

Next day, she caught the boat back to Crosslyon: with the bankruptcy and the arrival of so many auditors and auctioneers, the jetty was used now directly by the public boat. Phemie was waiting at the house. Was Sir Phelim well, or as well as could be expected?

'He's the same, my leddy. He took his broth, and I changed the sheets. He's comfortable, if ye were to go up.'

She went up, having meantime tidied herself and taken off her bonnet. She knelt down by the bed and let him put out his good hand to stroke her hair. He liked to do that, or now and again to touch her breast. So many men had touched her; she was used to it. It seemed a long time since Saturday. She heard Sir

Phelim try to speak.

'Play . . . harp.'

She kissed him, fetched it, and played gentle airs; not the wild music of former days. *Thus speaks the pride of former days, their glory's fulness o'er.* She remembered Mrs Smillie and her falsetto singing. She began to sing herself, knowing it would please him. All of her days were spent, after all, in pleasing others. She was a vessel, no more; but with a heart, beating still, as once at Tara.

Holy Joe was still savouring his remembered pleasure next day, and the day after, in fact, it would sustain him through the week. He diverted himself by the reminder that Brabazon couldn't possibly know all of it; the purchase, for a knockdown price, of the white elephant Crosslyon had become, with the view, later on, of turning it into an hotel, maybe with pleasure-boats; but not yet. It was not, truth to tell, that money was short; the Deccan cotton waved high, and he possessed enough rolling stock to convey it by means of his own transport across India when the time was ripe, and prices high enough; it took maybe a year or two to get folk used to the notion of a different source of raw material from the one they were in the habit of. There was a famine in Lancashire, they said, and no employment. Folk there were starving. He himself was not, having invested up here in the name of a foreign company he had meantime floated on the strength of a predictable future. A man had to keep his ear to the ground. He, Sproat, had anonymously bought and donated Orde's paddle-steamer to a grateful city, while seeing to it that the anonymity remained somewhat thin. That had maybe helped him in his final civic election. He glorified in the name of bailie. The position still gave him juridical rights of two kinds, the civil and the criminous variety. Nevertheless it gave him greater pleasure to rival McPhail in his amatory exploits than to see him ejected from his charge by the church authorities. What breasts young Brabazon had! He could handle those as well as the minister.

Sproat stretched himself, savouring the memory of her body, possessed by him, now, to a degree that levelled her with the humblest mill-girl. Aphrodite! To lie with her was like plunging into the heart of a rose. Nevertheless he would not risk marrying her when Sir Phelim died, as must happen soon. To ally himself, in his position, with the widow of a bankrupt would give the wrong impression. He would continue to possess the rose's heart till its petals fell, and keep silent on the matter thereafter.

* * *

In fact, Sunday afternoons were a revenge more intense than Sproat knew. Lady Orde.

Lady Muck. The minister's whore. He, Sproat, could make her sing for the supper he charitably provided day by day. Despite her loathing of him, which he knew of well enough and which itself stimulated him, he could cause her at times to like it; so he assured himself.

There was one minor worry; twice, by now, in course of proceedings, he'd leaked his condom. It didn't usually happen; he was prudent as a rule. However, the luscious flesh was like no other, a ripe peach as he'd foreseen, tempting any man beyond continence. In any case—the small mouth permitted itself a narrow smile—they could always blame the minister.

* * *

'Amy, fetch me the bundle of crochet hooks; they are tied with tape in the second top drawer of the escritoire.'

The indestructible Mrs McKitterick had fallen and broken her hip, and since then Amy had had to become even more of her slave than previously, fetching and carrying, wiping the aspidistra with milk—it was said by some to block the pores, however—and generally being at beck and call. The good lady herself lay on a sofa, in plaster, and would be there for some weeks. At least Amy had the downstairs bed alone.

She vanished into the parlour, where the escritoire sat near the window, and opened the drawer. As happens with things that are seldom used, the bundle of hooks had rolled to the back. Separating them out revealed a pile of papers, at the top of which Amy saw a letter addressed to herself. It had been opened. She took it out, the crochet hooks—Louisa had taken up the occupation out of ennui—still in her hand. Amy set the hooks down, and drew the letter out of its envelope. At first, she couldn't understand the signature. James Macrae.

'Amy.' Louisa had remembered that certain compromising material might be in the drawer; but was unable to get there to do anything about it. She called through to ask if the hooks had been found.

There was no answer. Amy was no longer in the parlour. She had hurried upstairs, to the attic and privacy. On the way she met Nancy Purdie.

'Go down and see to my mother,' she said. Mama could think what she liked. Amy kept the letter pressed against her breast. She would read it and re-read it, in enough peace to think. It had been sent four years ago. He'd written, after all. If she had known, she would have answered at once. He must have been waiting for a reply, and when none came hadn't written again. Mama—

Amy thrust the letter in the housewife she

wore. She would keep it always. She went then to the nursery, where the children were. They were both there, playing with coloured blocks. She sat down and watched them for some time, a prey to changing feelings. He'd had a son by Purdie, and she'd felt bitter. Now, it didn't seem to matter in some way. He'd written. She would write back, now, hoping against hope that it was not too late, that he could still be found in that vast country. Surely his red head would be known and remembered in passing, and a letter would be sent on.

Purdie had come back. 'Mrs McKitterick says you're to go down.'

'Tell her that I have a letter to write,' said Amy firmly. Her stomach no longer felt weak at disobeying Mama. Mama had betrayed her. She found writing-things and sat down in a place by herself, and when the letter was finished went out and posted it. Like the one that had come, it was carefully phrased; anybody could read it.

* * *

It was four months before a reply came. During that time she had maintained her silence. Louisa had grimly crocheted an afghan in coloured wools, and it was almost finished. Soon she'd be up and about again, and one could no longer rely on not being pried into, and letters taken.

However, this one came.

Ontario, 5th Jan

Dear Madam

Yours arrived safe, but I has to say Red Jim, as we called him not being able to say his name, is dead. He was killed by a big pine what fell on him up in Alberta. We think it was beavers, they eats away the low bark. His spine was broke, but he didn't die at once. I was there, and I remember he says, 'Tell Amy,' then he died without saying more. We didn't know who Amy was till yours came. I'm very sorry Madam. We liked him, all on us. We beried him and put up a cross, thats in the forest.

He remained hers respectfully, J. Brownrigg.

Amy felt the tears rise. They overflowed and poured down her cheeks. She didn't want to see Mama, or speak to her again. She fled upstairs and once more met Purdie, coming out of the nursery; the woman looked after the two children very well. She saw Amy, and the letter in her hand, and stretched out her own.

'If there's trouble, and I don't presume—' Presume was a word she'd learned from the old bitch; it meant mind your manners. Amy suddenly sobbed aloud and said to her, 'He's dead. You had a child by him, so you ought to be told. Here, read for yourself.' She knew Purdie could read and write, not like many servants.

The woman read the letter and handed it back quietly. Then she said, 'I think you had best know the truth, Mrs McPhail.'

Later, having heard everything, Amy went to where the red-haired boy was, took him in her thin arms and hugged him to her. This was her son, her son!

Bath Street, 21 April

Dear Uncle Julius

I think you know about my son, Edward. May I bring him to you, and may I stay with you myself? I can no longer live with my mother, and you were kind to me as a child. I would give you no trouble. You would like Eddie greatly, and he would grow up knowing you.

Your affectionate great-niece
Amy McPhail

Amy then went to her husband's study, stood facing him, and told him that his child was a daughter, born to him by way of Nancy Purdie; and that her own was the child of her lover, who was dead. 'I want to take Eddie away,' she said. 'My great-uncle in the north will rear him and see him educated. I want to be with them both for as long as I live. I mean nothing to you, not even by now as the mother of your child. Will you give me money with which to travel? I will not trouble you again.'

He was silent, then went to a drawer and

took out enough coins, and gave them to her. ‘It is not for me to reproach you,’ he told her. ‘I have enough reproach of my own.’

That Sunday, there was only Purdie in the pew, for many reasons.

* * *

The old man in the Highland lodge was very old indeed now, his hair, still thick, as white as snow, his frame thin as a bone. He would sit all day in the room whose window looked out on the moors, where he no longer went out after grouse: they were brought to him, plucked and roasted, in season. Hour by hour, as the days passed, he would look instead at the full-length portrait hanging on the wall, of his long-dead son in the dark tartan of the 42nd, butchered together with the rest at Sebastopol. Then he would turn his head, in which the worldly lids drooped over eyes that had seen many things, to where the guru sat, cross-legged and half-naked as usual except for a loin-cloth. No one ever saw Ahur eat or drink; his strength came from elsewhere. The old man spoke now, his voice tired.

‘Have you no word yet? Is there no voice for me?’ He had hoped, ever since the news came long ago, that his son would send for him, that it would be time to die. However, Amy had written lately; he would like to see the child who would inherit all he had. The guru spoke.

‘There is no voice for yourself yet, but for another. She is coming soon, with the boy who has been born, as I told you. It will not be long. I can see them in the Great Mirror. In an hour they will be here, and will not leave again.’

That was true; for as long as he lived, Amy could stay, with the boy, and as she had said would do no harm. He did not ask further questions of Ahur, but wondered how much time more would be left to Amy to live; her child was young.

He heard them arrive then, the carriage having brought them from the station at Inverness. Julius waited in his chair and did not go out to greet them; his bones were old, like the rest of him.

They entered, the thin woman and the boy, whom she led by the hand. He was old enough to walk confidently. Amy’s great-uncle greeted her, noting how she had changed, and Eddie wandered off to gaze up at the portrait of the young man dead many years.

‘Sodger,’ he said. He had seen them marching in Glasgow, one day when Purdie took him down to the High Street. He missed Purdie, who had always looked after him till his mother, as he had to call her now, took him away. However, he had a phlegmatic nature and mother was kind, as Purdie had been. This place, the brown naked guru, and the old man in the chair, were like nothing he had ever seen or imagined, but he liked the portrait of the young soldier in the kilt best by far. It was what he would like to become, as he already knew.

'Sodger,' he said again, and Amy apologised. 'He has been left with servants, and his speech is theirs,' she said. 'He will grow out of it.'

'Come to me,' said old Julius to the child, who delighted him already. 'Would you indeed like to be a soldier when you are grown?' He would educate this fine boy, would arrange for him to be placed in a worthy regiment. It could be Nicholas over again, without the Crimea. However, he knew he would not see this second boy grow to manhood.

The guru remained silent. He could see mud and blood, and knew that this child would live to take part in a far greater war, with unnumbered deaths, than had been the case at Sebastopol and Inkerman. Whether young Eddie would live through it or not he could not tell. He could, however, hear a young man's voice calling for the woman, telling Amy to come soon. Ahur raised his shaven head, and spoke.

'There is one who calls always for you,' he told her. 'You will go to him within the year. His name is Seumas, and he is the father of your son.'

The old survivor of the Honourable East India Company hardly heeded him, though Amy did, and felt herself uplifted in air, the world left behind. Great-uncle Julius meantime had the little boy on his knee, and was ruffling his red hair amiably.

CHAPTER THREE

Brabazon lay alone on the floor of the clock-chamber, listening to the eternal loud tick, tock. It seemed to be ticking away her life, and within moments the great chime would come, deafening her; it was unsafe, she knew, to stay as near. Nevertheless while she lay here, it was still the place where she had lain with Aeneas McPhail; and it brought him near, as if he knew she was thinking of him, remembering, on the same floor. That first time they had come together had been inevitable, like a magnet meeting metal; since then, she couldn't claim as much, it had been arranged by them both, the meetings in the coach-house were planned, their shared delight deliberate and fleeting; spoilt forever in her own awareness of what must happen next day, at the silent mill. She thrust that from her mind, and again willed McPhail to come to her in his thoughts; was he writing now, at his study desk, or maybe visiting the parish? The old women would talk and talk, and make tea. He himself didn't have to say much. He was never a man of many words, even while making love. She knew his mind and soul, and thought with longing of his body; his great powerful man's physique, furred with black hair at the chest and arms, and also the lover's place; that she longed for now, with an intensity that made her clutch at her own breasts. Tick, tock; tick, tock. She could see the great clock-face itself from where she lay; it was overlaid in blue enamel, the hands and figures in bright brass, and the name of the Birmingham maker and the date, 1859, showed below; oh, she knew it all, it wasn't the first time she had come up here alone, to remember, remember, and cleanse her soul. Love was a cleansing thing; what happened at the mill wasn't, and yet her body had grown accustomed to what it had not before known, the rising of foreseeable lust despite herself, despite the stubby hands, Sproat's gruntings, her loathing of him. He was a pig, the bailie; and everything of the kind was kept furtive, he would be careful never to be seen with her in public, even here; when he came, it was to visit Sir Phelim, for what that was now worth. He had ruined the dying man, ruined them both in some way she, herself, didn't understand; it concerned the rise and fall of cotton prices, and the American war and the famine in Lancashire. Brabazon thought again of McPhail; and the great clock whirred and chimed then, once, twice, three times. She put her fingers in her ears, still lying on the floor, looking at the shallow carved balcony which surrounded the clock-chamber; if anyone wanted to throw themselves down, they would die. She didn't want to, in spite of everything. She wanted to live, and love, and be loved.

The last chime died down into an echo, and she became aware that Phemie the maid was standing there watching her gravely. Brabazon sat up, disturbed at having been found in such a pose, lying on the ground; it must seem odd to a servant.

'What is it?' she said with unusual sharpness. The woman made a slight bob. 'My leddy, puir Sir Phelim's deid. He canna ha'e heard the clock strike three. He died in his sleep; as ye ken, he hasna waukened often ower the last days, except when we brocht the broth till him.' Her speech had broadened into the vernacular, showing that she was upset. Brabazon hastened to rise, smoothing her hair and skirts; and went down. It didn't matter now whether or not Phemie wondered why she was here. She should have been with poor Sir Phelim as usual; perhaps he'd tried to call out before he died, even in sleep. He'd always wanted her near him.

* * *

His face was already smoothing over, the sparse grey hair echoing its death-pallor. Brabazon kissed his cheek; it was already growing cold. She turned to Phemie, who had come down behind her.

'You must send for the doctor,' she said. That had to be done, she knew, at a death.

There would be a great many other things to do. The first was to send word to the newspapers. The second, and she did it at once, was to write to Aeneas. He would of course conduct the service. For once, it was correct to send for him. She longed for his presence more than anything in the world, even standing here looking down at her dead husband. She wondered if many, by now, would trouble to attend the funeral.

* * *

There was no doubt of that; all the way down to Row church, along the roads, the working folk stood, the men with their cloth caps in their hands, bareheaded out of respect; Sir Phelim had once been a good employer to them. The hearse passed by, and some of the women wept, maybe for no other reason than that it was the thing to do; everyone was sad for the young widow, but ladies didn't attend funerals even in a carriage. The majesty of bailiedom was however present, in the form of Joseph Sproat, who it was already whispered meant to take over Crosslyon in some way; maybe there would be work again in the house and gardens. As many as might crowded into the small church, and later out to the graveyard where Sir Phelim was laid to rest. It was whispered, likewise, that Bailie Sproat would pay for a stone memorial, maybe next year, giving the earth time to settle.

* * *

The young widow herself sat in the winter garden, where the palms were not quite what they had formerly been although she kept them watered. Heat could no longer be afforded, and the camellia was dead. Beside her, likewise in mourning but without weepers such as old Mrs Swords had seen fit to wear though Brabazon did not, sat Mrs McIntyre, the headmistress of the seminary. Sir Phelim in his day having been a school governor, she had felt it incumbent on her to come down, not to attend church—ladies didn't—but to sit with the widow, who after all had been a pupil once. They had said very little, and Mrs McIntyre decided not to put forward meantime the notion she had had of asking dear Brabazon, once the immediate mourning was over, perhaps to come and give harp and singing lessons to the young ladies for a small fee. It was known she had very little on which to live. Moreover Miss Potts, who saw to hair-washing and put out the dormitory lights at night, was incontinently leaving to be married. It would be possible to offer Brabazon a full-time post, but her remembered lack of submissiveness made that a prospect which must be considered for rather longer. One would write. It would certainly be a social step upwards to be able to say that Lady Orde oversaw certain accomplishments at the school. The whole thing needed reflection, and here was the tall form of the minister, returned from the service. No doubt he would give spiritual consolation. Mrs McIntyre rose.

'It is fitting that Sir Phelim was so widely remembered. I am sure the service was well conducted,' she remarked, and turned to Brabazon. 'I hope, my dear, to be in touch with you rather sooner than has been the case lately: I believe it is two years since we encountered one another. Good day, Mr McPhail; remember me to your mother-in-law.' It was known, as such things always are, that his wife had not been seen at the manse for some time now, for whatever reason. That did not seem a satisfactory state of things.

* * *

I should have offered her tea, and I didn't, Brabazon thought; and held out her arms. McPhail gathered her in his own, and they clung; the headmistress, turning to look in farewell through the glass from the outer path, decided finally that the offer of a situation would not do. In fact, she would discontinue the hire of the carriage which permitted supervised weekly attendance at Oakdale services. No breath of scandal must be risked in connection with her school; it was after all her livelihood. She reflected grimly that there would be less of a resulting harvest in McPhail's collection-plate than formerly. He should act with more dignity in his position.

McPhail was looking down at Brabazon's bright head in its black veil, laid with relief against his coat. 'Take me away,' she was saying. 'I don't want to stay here alone. I'm afraid.' Sproat might come, she knew; and the ticking of the clock brought terror now, and the thought of the grave.

He had intended, now Sir Phelim was gone, taking her back with him to the manse in any case. There could be no complaints, as Louisa McKitterick's presence lent respectability. Nevertheless he was puzzled, and showed it.

'My dearest, you told my mother-in-law that you had tea with Mrs McIntyre on Sunday afternoons, yet she said just now you had not met one another for two years.'

He had spoken gently, but saw her whiten, then burst into tears against his coat. 'Do not ask me yet,' she said. 'I will tell you when I may, but not now, not here.'

'Come,' he said; whatever was causing her distress must not sever them. 'I have told Phemie to get ready your things,' he told her. 'You will bring her with you, and you will both return with me now in the hired carriage.' It could not have turned out more conveniently. Brabazon should not go back to the coach-house, he had decided. She should sleep every night in his arms.

*   *   *

It so happened that the boat the headmistress caught at Crosslyon pier was the same which brought back certain eminent persons earlier from Row, having attended the funeral service. As there had been no subsequent provision of refreshments, they had felt themselves in need of a dram. This having been achieved, they were making their way back to town somewhat less discreetly than usual. Among the company was Holy Joe Sproat and also, for he had business to transact in Glasgow, Smillie, Justice of the Peace, married to the falsetto with the frizzed blonde hair. She was, of course, left at home; but as Mrs McIntyre herself got on board the gentlemen became extremely gallant, raising their tall hats and greeting her with a familiarity which would not have been the case had they been entirely sober.

'Poor Old Phelim. He was the salt of the earth. Nae doubt his young widow will find herself a man.'

Smillie turned then to Mrs McIntyre, who he knew by awestruck sight already as one of his daughters had briefly attended the seminary to be finished. 'Ye were with Lady Orde, I dare say,' he said. 'What will become of her? Has she ony kin living?' He remembered the delectable sight and sound of Brabazon singing *The Harp that Once,* second verse, after Muriel had shrilled the first; one had got used to that. 'Will she give harp lessons, maybe, or singing lessons? They say she did well wi' Madame Padovani.' He was, of course, informed.

'She'll sing for her supper, some way,' put in the bailie coarsely. The men in the party knew what he meant, and burst out laughing in an unseemly fashion. Mrs McIntyre, who did not know such things, put in primly that Lady Orde was being taken care of by the minister. This produced more laughter. 'He'll be consoling her wi' mair nor religion, I doubt,' said the J.P. slyly.

Bailie Sproat was not amused; he felt rage rise, and was determined to be spiteful. If the small house at Hogganfield he had already taken remained unoccupied, he had wasted his money. To think that she had gone with McPhail already! It was hardly decent. They would be travelling by road. 'He will be consoling her, certainly,' he remarked smoothly. 'It's well known he visits her on Saturdays, at that wee coach-house they used to maintain.' He refrained from adding that was his own property now, like everything else. Brabazon Orde should no longer have the use of it, or his goodwill in anything. The small mouth pursed itself, feeling the benefit of the whisky wear off. He knew Smillie had heard him, and would retail the story to Mrs Smillie, who would relay it in turn to Glasgow in general. As for the schoolmistress, she had turned away, saying she preferred to go down to the cabin. They went on with their talk more freely without her. By the end of the voyage, Brabazon's reputation was in shreds, and so was the minister's.

* * *

All of it suited Sproat well enough. He had for some time intended a voyage to visit Hyderabad to inspect his ripening cotton harvest; it paid to show them out there that personal attention was given, no profits creamed off to middlemen. It would mean an absence of thirteen weeks, but it was worth it. He would leave a reliable clerk at the Glasgow office. When he returned, he would take up the threads again; that meant wool and flax, as well as Brabazon once more. By then, she would be glad enough of his protection; other women of her class would have ostracised her after the talk on the boat had spread. As for McPhail, it was better to be seen to have nothing to do with what must happen; the man's eventual and certain disgrace. It had been a timely resignation of his own from the post of session-clerk, saying with truth that he had other business. As an elder, he could still sit in judgment.

*   *   *

McPhail carried Brabazon, in her weeds, up the steps and in over the threshold at Bath Street like a bride, the maid Phemie following stolidly with her mistress's small baggage and her own. Once there, she was told to wait; Purdie appeared with a cup of tea.

'If ye are staying, maybe, I'd be glad if ye were to look to puir Mrs McKitterick. She has a broken hip, and they say ye nursed old Sir Phelim very well.'

Phemie was flattered, as had been intended; but said she ought perhaps to ask Lady Orde, who would be tired from the journey and the long time of worry there had been. 'It's been a while since Sir Phelim took ill.' She spoke uncertainly; it was the first time she and Nancy Purdie had set eyes on one another, and Phemie could see that the other young woman had some sort of authority in the manse. Maybe she was the housekeeper. There didn't seem any sign of a Mrs McPhail.

Nancy said firmly that Lady Orde was resting. In fact she had glimpsed, out of the corner of her eye, the minister carry Brabazon straight up to the first-floor bedroom himself. Unless a maid was sent for, there was no call to disturb them. Later Purdie went up silently to the nursery, where only one child, her own daughter, remained. On the way she passed the bedroom door, and from beyond heard what Joe Sproat had once found to assail his ears at the clock chamber; a woman's moans of pleasure. Well, it was still the day of the funeral, and for Mr McPhail's sake the fewer folk who knew the better. Nancy was already well acquainted with conditions at the coach-house, took no umbrage and never had.

Over the days that passed Phemie settled down, if that was how anyone could describe it, as Louisa's house-slave, carrying out the tasks Amy had once done, including the winding of wool for knitting and crochet. It was slightly easier now than it had been then, as Louisa herself had grown querulous with shock at her daughter's departure, and in fact confided a good deal to the sympathetic ear of this trained woman servant from Crosslyon. Phemie was glad enough of the employment; until things were settled down-river, there wasn't much there for women; the men could always find work at the iron-foundries and shipyards. Looking after Mrs McKitterick at least gave her, Phemie Denny, a roof over her head, food, and some money, not to mention the sights of Glasgow on her day off. The arrangement worked very well.

* * *

Bailie Sproat, not yet departed, was emerging from a councillors' meeting when he was accosted by one of them, a man who was likewise one of the elders at Oakdale parish.

'Good day to ye, bailie. It's been better weather.' He carried a black umbrella in case it was not. As everyone knows, this is the best way of keeping the rain away.

He then remarked that there was a wheen gossip about the long absence of Mrs McPhail. It was said she was in the north with a relative. 'It's time she was back,' remarked the elder. 'Her duty is to look after the manse and the minister, not to go gallimaufring off by herself. Someone should speak to McPhail; he's too lenient, having an eye always to his sermons. That's as it should be, but other things they say are not, or not for the time.'

Sproat put in deliberately that Mrs McPhail had maybe found her place taken. The elder made a shocked face, then gave away the fact that, like most, he knew all about it.

'Yon Lady Orde. I've heard about it from time to time.' He shut a prudent upper lip over the lower, disguising his undoubted dentures. Sproat said, 'That affair went on for long enough down at the coach-house, but it is a different matter keeping her abovestairs at the manse. No wife could be expected to put up with it,' he added piously. Bachelor as he was and intended to remain—he liked his freedom—he knew well enough the state of affairs in general; men had a wife at home and a mistress, or an occasional prostitute, elsewhere. It was unheard-of to bring fallen women into the house.

'She comes to church,' said the elder. 'There would have been a time when she'd have been put to stand on a stool of repentance.'

'And the minister on another? That would do small good to the respect shown to the cloth in general.'

'It is a long time since I heard that phrase used,' replied the elder, and they walked in silence for some moments out of the old part of town towards the new. Sproat tried to remember the results of the late meeting, which had concerned unabated crime in the Saltmarket. He was unable to recall what they had decided, if anything, to do about it; even the police dared not go there at nights yet, with their new powers.

In fact his mind was chiefly filled with a gnawing hunger which seldom left him; the unslaked desire for Brabazon's lovely and, for the present, unattainable flesh. *I can have your fancy man pulled down out of the pulpit, and sent to beg his bread.* Should he say it in her ear, on a Sunday? They all came; including Nancy Purdie, who didn't seem, these days, to bring her wee boy with her; maybe he was getting out of hand. A child needed discipline. Sproat consoled himself with thoughts of what he would do to punish Brabazon in such ways once he had her lying under him again. *Warm tae't, lass, or I'll skelp your bum.* That and other hopeful images consoled him briefly now, walking away from Jamaica Street and the river.

*   *   *

'I think I am going to have a child,' Brabazon murmured against McPhail, lying together as they were now every night; he would stay with her till dawn, then leave and go to his own bed so that the maids would think it had been slept in. He heard her at once with joy and pain. Certainly it might have been expected, they were all in all to one another, she was his delight, his inspiration, flesh of his flesh. Nevertheless the thought of yet another child to be given an identity disturbed him. 'My dear love, are you certain?'

He kissed her tenderly, and she began to sob. 'Certain of that—if it were only that!' Suddenly, she told him about Sproat and his usage of her, how he had sent the carriage for her by habit on Sundays, threatening to tell the Oakdale session about his, McPhail's, own Saturday visits if she didn't come. 'I didn't want to spoil those. I didn't want you to be in danger either.'

'He did this?' He was horrified, then enraged. 'I'll kill him.' He clutched her closer to him; she was a hurt creature, frightened now, he knew, of going out alone. He hadn't been certain why; now, he understood. He felt her hand, a flower still, stroke his cheek. Sproat had gone abroad; when he returned, he should answer for his actions with his life. He swore it as a Highlander, a McGregor, a McPhail.

'Do not touch him. If anything happens to you, what will become of me? It is surely your child, he was always what he called careful.' She began to laugh and cry bitterly, soaking his nightshirt. He downed his rising anger, and promised, in the end, that he would not after all touch Sproat meantime, though his instinct was to choke the life out of the man next time he set eyes on him.

The next time was, of course, after the boat docked from India. Sproat was punctilious in his morning attendance on the first Sunday following his return. He placed himself where he could eye Brabazon, mentally undressing her where she sat. It seemed a certainty that her waist was thicker by now than two hands' span. Well, he would keep out of the matter. In any case it was rumoured that she had settled in at the manse; several of the more respectable families had rented pews elsewhere in the city. Sproat himself had elected to rent the former Orde one here; it was expensive, and suited his civic position. Some other body would no doubt be going round with the plate.

He passed his tongue between his lips. Looking at her, even as she was now, roused certain sensations in him. It was more than possible the minister would be asked to leave, though such matters were officially voluntary and rarely happened. He, Sproat, would certainly express his own distaste at the existing situation as soon as an opportunity occurred to do so discreetly. Aphrodite. Would this Eros-birth be soon enough to blame the late Sir Phelim? It would be a tight fit. No doubt they would try. One way and another, the prospect was diverting.

*　　*　　*

It was perhaps in time for that, perhaps not. The weeks dragged past, and Brabazon began to be torn between her fear of being discovered and the need for her, without fail, to be present in church to listen to McPhail's preaching. She had once suggested to him that she might stay at home—the first-floor room had become this by now, Purdie brought meals up on a tray—and the puzzled and hurt look in his dark eyes changed her mind. She laughed, saying she hadn't meant it; of course she would come in the carriage to hear him preach. It was no great trial, after all, to sit there with Purdie and the little girl, attend the service and be brought smoothly back again. Nevertheless she was aware that the church was increasingly empty; McPhail preached to unrented pews where once the prosperous of town had sat each week. Perhaps it was the cotton famine, which seemed to have made everyone poorer. Even Mrs McIntyre no longer brought her young ladies.

Once, at the manse, she told herself not to be foolish about meeting others; she certainly ought to look in and enquire for Mrs McKitterick, who lay on her sofa behind closed doors on the ground floor, off the hall. Brabazon by then was growing heavy, and flung a shawl over herself, then went down; a sound of voices came from inside, and she turned the handle and ventured in, immediately regretting it. One of the visitors was Mrs Smillie, who'd come to dinner at Crosslyon that time and tried to sing. The other was an Oakdale woman parishioner. Both of them rose at once and made their excuses, going out by the door with stiff backs turned to reveal narrow crinolines, and no word spoken.

Brabazon was left facing Louisa McKitterick, who said coldly, 'You should not be in this house. You are a sinful woman.'

The hazel eyes were hard as pebbles. Brabazon turned and left her.

CHAPTER FOUR

After that she ceased to see anyone, or even to attend church; that was where those women gossiped. She told McPhail only that she was afraid the birth would come when she was out in the carriage, or in the pew. Even he understood that it was growing near. He still came and slept with her; she passed the days in waiting, waiting for him to come, lying on the sofa and brushing out her own long hair. She still didn't know what to expect when the baby came; Purdie had only said it happened. Brabazon hoped McPhail would be there to hold her in his arms. She couldn't picture herself with a baby. After it was born, perhaps she would be able to lace herself up again and look like other people.

* * *

Louisa McKitterick lay frowning after the two women, and that Brabazon Orde, had gone. She had done her utmost to spread the assumption that Brabazon's coming child was the late husband's. She herself knew nothing about the ultimate physical state of Sir Phelim, and very few people had seen him after he had lost all his money. It would retrieve the good name of Oakdale, the Bath Street manse, Mr

McPhail and, indirectly, herself, if such a conclusion could be generally accepted. In other words, the sooner the birth took place the better: it lent weight to the story. She sent for Purdie, asked her certain questions, and was satisfied. She had heard, meantime, the minister come in, and as usual go straight upstairs to his mistress. It was reprehensible; but the more of that that took place the better; it brought it on, one understood. She sent Purdie upstairs to listen, then to come down again.

'Is he in bed with her?' she asked bluntly. Nancy flushed.

'Ay.' It was the same always: they were happy, the minister and his beautiful lady.

'Well, you must keep me constantly informed. I only regret that I am not in a state to supervise matters personally. You may tell Phemie to come in.' She had sent Phemie away, as not properly entitled to hear such a conversation; Purdie, on the other hand, had a child of her own.

Purdie ascended the stairs again quietly, and went straight to the nursery, where little Phoebe, as they'd called her, was playing by herself with the coloured blocks. No doubt the child was solitary now Eddie had gone to the north. If this other lived and grew, it would be company for Phoebe. Nobody asked how many children were in a nursery, or taken out walking. The beautiful creature on the first floor, with her distended body and tiny feet, didn't seem to care about anything but her lover, to be lifted in McPhail's strong arms and carried once again to the bed. Otherwise she spent the days lying in her wrapper on the sofa, brushing out her hair or else lying in Mrs Amy's bath. By now, she was too heavy safely to risk it. Purdie was reminded in some way of fruit that couldn't ripen, lacking the sun.

* * *

Like most young ladies from the likes of Mrs McIntyre's, or even from their mothers' own houses, Lady Orde herself knew nothing about the pains of birth. On being asked, Nancy had avoided mention of them; bad enough when they came, without looking forward to it. 'They come out in the end,' was all she'd said; adding that she herself was still alive and so was Mrs Amy.

'What happened to the little boy who used to be with you? He was yours, was he not?'

'Ay. He's in the north parts.' She didn't mention Mrs Amy then either.

It was increasingly difficult by now for Nancy to remember which child was whose. She'd been fond of both, and would be fond of this one when it came; she liked children. It was to be hoped Lady Orde would come through it safely. It was a mercy the old bitch herself lay downstairs with her broken leg.

She'd maybe have smothered whichever it turned out to be this time, or even Lady Orde. It could be said easily enough *she'd* died at the birth, poor beautiful lady. A great many things could be easily said; too easily.

* * *

McPhail was in fact with Brabazon when the labour started, early one Sunday morning. She bit her lip and said nothing of it, knowing he must put in an appearance at church. 'Hurry back,' was all she whispered, and he kissed her and promised; watching his tall figure go out of the door she felt, as always, her limbs grow weak with love.

Purdie had not gone with him today. She knew, from the look of her ladyship, that it wouldn't be long; and yesterday she had gone downstairs and asked Phemie, who never came up now, if she would help. Phemie flushed, and said Mrs McKitterick had told her that if she took anything at all to do with it, she would be shown the door. 'I'll boil some water,' she said, 'and leave it on the landing.' She offered to look after little Phoebe if she was sent downstairs; the child hadn't, of course, gone by herself in the carriage to Oakdale with nobody to look after her.

Purdie took her daughter grimly down; after all the old bitch was supposed to be her grandmother. Nobody knew how much or how little Louisa McKitterick's silences meant. She had kept one long ago in Manchester, and would keep one here. As far as this coming child was concerned, it was Sir Phelim Orde's. That was the law, for a baby born within the year, even though the mother's husband was dead and the woman a widow.

Purdie went back upstairs to find that the waters had burst and that Lady Orde was standing there crying, not knowing what to do next. 'I'll walk ye up and down,' said Nancy firmly. 'That brings it on. Don't fret, my leddy; I ken what to dae.' She'd done it for herself, after all, in Nile Street, that time the old bitch came later and switched the births.

* * *

McPhail hardly knew what he delivered that day from the pulpit. After the service he hurried back as promised, and straight upstairs. By then Brabazon and the servant were still walking up and down the room, past Amy's bath of many taps, and being a man he thought things were not too bad and he would go and have some food. He kissed Brabazon again and told her he would come back; there were some papers to see to. By the time he returned, the labour had started and went on thereafter for many hours. Half frenzied, McPhail drove down to the evening service and back, again not knowing what he had said to such folk as still came. By the time of his second return the child was not yet born, and Brabazon had become a little howling animal, lying on the bed with Purdie hovering about her. He thanked God for Purdie. The woman turned her head.

'Maybe ye will fetch up the can of hot water now, minister; it's on the landing.' It was an unheard-of thing to ask him to do, but he obeyed, not seeing for himself Nancy's urgent reason; a small hand with stubby fingers, dangling at last from the labouring mother's parts by its arm.

Nancy knew. A cross-birth; and Sproat had got at her, with less than his accustomed prudence. Maybe at this rate the child would be born dead. Nevertheless she, Purdie, did what she might to correct it; such things were however painful, and Brabazon cried out in continued agony. At last, after many hours of turning by hand and straining fearfully, the child was born; a girl, with fair hair. Purdie tried to cover it up when the minister came, but what was the use? He'd see it sooner or later; a rat's face, like its father, and it had all but killed my lady. The minister had knelt down and taken her again in his arms now, exhausted as she was: the two of them as usual having eyes for nothing but one another.

* * *

He had in fact come up just in time. Presently Brabazon gave a little cry against him, said, 'Ah, the pain,' and put up her hand to stroke his face, then the hand fell powerless back on the covers. Her eyes, still gazing at him with great love, filmed over. He had seen death often, but could not believe that she, his life, was dead. He stayed there kissing and fondling her hands and calling her name, till Purdie, who had put the baby aside in its wrappings, came gently and led him away. 'She's dead, poor soul,' she said to him. 'There's things to be done, and the doctor should be sent for.'

*　　*　　*

Louisa McKitterick had some time previously begun to stump about downstairs with a stick; the healed leg would always, to her annoyance, be a different height from the other. She called out for Phemie, who didn't come at once; she was with that dark-haired child, in the further room. 'Come when I tell you,' called Louisa, and the door opened and the minister stood there, eyes blazing in a cavernous face like a skull.

'The woman whom you called sinful is dead,' he said. 'You yourself will one day stand face to face with God, as she does now. You have lived here under this roof for long enough; take your gear by tomorrow, and go. Your maid will accompany you. You should have saved enough by now, by living here, to maintain yourself. This room will be occupied by Lady Orde's coffin. I prefer that you do not attend it, or her funeral.'

He turned and left. Well, it was short enough notice; she'd have to leave a few things for Phemie to collect later. Meantime, she could go to Muriel Smillie, who in any case would be agog to hear all that had happened. After that she would look in the papers for somewhere out of town to rent. It was true she'd saved something; Uncle Julius had continued to pay her the annuity he'd begun at the time of her husband's suicide. She would not, of course, go north to him and Amy; not for any consideration. The red-haired boy had, it was evident, come into his own, whether or not they knew who was his father.

* * *

McPhail had made up his mind to kill Sproat after all as soon as he saw the fluff of fair hair on the new child's head when Purdie carried it away. The agony Brabazon had undergone was the bailie's fault and no other's, and he should pay. McPhail had watched her die, and wished, looking down later on her calm, still face, that he could have her body cremated as had been done in ancient times, and carry the ashes always with him. However, it was not permitted now by law. He turned to Purdie, who was never far away.

'Cut me a lock of her hair,' he said, and went out of the room.

Purdie brought it to him later, the long curling tress of bright brown hair. He would wear it next his heart always. Having bestowed it, he walked out of the house and down to Sproat's city office. He would not kill the man quite yet; he knew already how he would do that, after the funeral.

Sproat greeted him with false friendliness, offering him a chair and whisky, both of which the minister declined. Still standing in front of the bailie's mahogany desk, he said, 'You may not yet know that Brabazon Orde is dead. As her executor, not that she had much to leave, I am asked by her to obtain certain personal possessions she left hidden at Crosslyon. The house is in your ownership and I consider it correct to ask you to come with me, at your convenience, to retrieve what I have been told of.'

'She should not have hidden anything,' said Sproat. 'The house is mine, and all contents were sold off following the bankruptcy. What are these things?'

'They are her personal possessions, as I said. You know her harp was left there, that is hers.'

Sproat laughed. 'It will make a piece of decoration at the hotel. They are not things desired by everyone, but I can make that use of it.'

He had shown no sorrow at news of Brabazon's death. Her flesh by now was cold, he was thinking, no longer to be desired and handled. McPhail looked like death himself. The bailie decided to humour him. 'Well, I can meet ye down there on Thursday at maybe four o'clock,' he said. 'I have some business to clear up in any case. Ye can uncover the mystery then, minister, and we can decide one way or the other about ownership.' It depended, he was thinking, on whether or not the intrinsic value was great; the sapphires, for instance, had fetched a good price, and as Sir Phelim's own purchase had been included in the objects for sale. One way and the other, it was worth going down.

* * *

The dead woman's coffin had been carried down to the ground-floor room at Bath Street. Louisa McKitterick and her belongings had gone. Nancy Purdie and the minister were left alone, staring down at the name and age on the closed lid. It had been young to die.

McPhail then said a strange thing. 'In old times they would hold what they called a wake for the dead, and sing all night, sometimes for two nights,' he said. 'I would give more than anything to hear her voice again. I did not ask her to sing to me often enough.'

No, ye were too busy in bed, the pair of ye, Nancy thought. Aloud she said comfortingly that Lady Orde would surely sing with the angels where she had gone. 'Maybe, but I cannot hear her,' said the minister.

She left him seated in his black clothes by the coffin, where he would remain until the funeral. Purdie didn't suppose many would come. The situation was well known to everybody, but of course not talked of openly, nothing was. She had a sudden longing for fresh air, away from the city fogs and soot and gossip, and the stench from the river. Maybe the minister would consider taking a holiday after he left his Oakdale charge; she knew by now he wouldn't stay in it. The well-found folk would come back to the parish church, no doubt, once he was gone. What would happen to her, Nancy, she didn't know. Maybe he wanted her with him, maybe he didn't. He was not, in any case, the kind of man who could do forever without a woman. That only happened in story-books. It wasn't for her to say anything; and at the moment, he was sad.

She wondered where it was the old bitch and Phemie had found to go. Later, she was to discover that there had been a rented house available very reasonably, newly furnished and advertised, at Hogganfield. That was where they had gone, away from the fogs and gossip and smells. Purdie envied them.

*　　　*　　　*

Phemie the erstwhile Crosslyon maid was an obedient creature without much imagination, but even she was aware that her own situation had changed, in essentials, twice. At first, she had been devoted to the beautiful young lady Sir Phelim had brought home as his bride. It was a pleasure to put out Lady Orde's different dresses, brush her marvellous hair, admire her jewels and the colourful silk bed-curtains with their fringes, where she slept. Phemie herself had always smoothed the bed in question after Sir Phelim and his lady spent their Sunday afternoons in a certain fashion, as married couples no doubt often did. After that, with Sir Phelim's illness and, at first, a hired nurse, Phemie had twice gone up to the Glasgow coach-house with young Lady Orde, and had been sent with spending-money to divert herself on Glasgow Green, being instructed not to return before a certain time. Once she had been early, had waited where the coach used to be kept and had seen the minister leave. Then, she'd thought nothing of it; but later on there had been the loss of all the money, and the hired nurse had gone, and she and Lady Orde and old Mrs Mackay had done the job of looking after Sir Phelim between them. She, Phemie, had taken to nursing well enough, though it was different from being a lady's maid; but she knew enough to know that it couldn't, by then, any longer be a marriage. Then, at Sir Phelim's death, she'd gone up to the clock-tower and found Lady Orde lying on the ground in a very odd manner, though granted she'd got up and come downstairs at once. One way and another it was possible to come to certain conclusions, and it was not possible, as Mrs McKitterick was saying now, that the child lately born was of course poor Sir Phelim's: few were aware of Sir Phelim's state over the last months. It seemed that the minister would adopt the baby, as well he might. Phemie's lips set disapprovingly. Lady Orde had been whisked away out of her own life ever since they both came up to Bath Street in the hired carriage after Sir Phelim's funeral, and the minister and Lady Orde gazing into one another's eyes all the way and saying nothing during the journey. She herself had felt remarkably in the way.

She wouldn't say anything, of course; she hadn't seen the new baby. Purdie was looking after it, as Purdie looked after everything. It was no longer anything to do with her, Euphemia Denny, strictly reared. It was better, though less pleasant, to settle down here with Mrs McKitterick in the new rented house. At least it meant a situation, and a reference later on.

* * *

McPhail arrived earlier at Crosslyon than he had intended, as he had expected the boat he took to go straight on as usual to Row. However, Sproat would undoubtedly have come down earlier still. Whether or not he had business to transact as he had stated, there was little doubt that he would try to lay his hands on whatever it was Brabazon had instructed the minister to find.

He would find nothing. In fact, the whole story was a fabrication, and as he went along the path McPhail examined his conscience, found it entirely clear, and realised that, at that rate and with one thing and another, he was certainly damned. With what he hoped was about to happen, he would no doubt be hanged first as well.

They said sinners seldom recognised their own state of sin. His own brand of theology maintained that some were saved and others not. He had at times doubted it: but at that rate, nothing he did now would ensure his rescue from damnation, and as well be hanged for a sheep. He approached the lodge, then the garden, which drooped sadly; Sproat had not yet begun his glorifications for the intended hotel. The place had an abandoned air, and he could hear the clock tick from here; tick, tock; tick, tock. That was where he intended to avenge Brabazon: in the clock-chamber, as the hour struck.

Sproat greeted him with an air of one who is as usual very busy and has been disturbed, but will agree to be civil to the interloper. He led McPhail through the great empty hall; that and the corridors retained their long crimson carpets, these not having been found suitable to sell when cut up. The two men's footsteps therefore sounded softly as they went past Brabazon's harp, standing to one side near a window. Its cover was off and one string was frayed. Sproat dragged his stubby fingers across the rest contemptuously, causing the ghost of sad music.

'It is possible that there is nothing here,' he said pleasantly. 'Our Brab liked her joke, maybe, eh, minister?'

The ugly shortening of Brabazon's beautiful name, the possessive familiarity, the very touching of the harp itself, increased McPhail's anger. He would have no mercy on this man. He did not reply.

'Where is it that we are to go?' enquired Sproat, still jocose.

'The clock-chamber.' Tick, tock; tick, tock. It was a few minutes yet to the hour.

Sproat frowned. 'The clock's value was assessed, and by the time it was taken out it would have been worth very little. In any case it is a feature, though I believe I will silence the ticking; it will get on folks' nerves.'

'What I have come for will be found when the whirring begins for the chime,' said

McPhail. He added that he had exact instructions, which after all was true enough.

They ascended the carpeted stairs. Memory crowded into the minister's mind, almost blotting out what he had come to do; that first day of all, they had come up here together, and had fallen to the floor in one another's arms without knowing it. Never again, never again, no more, no more; a coronach. Where had he heard that? He remembered; at his sister Jessie's death at Kilbeg, long ago.

They entered the high chamber; with the emptiness below, the ticking sounded intolerably loud. McPhail laid his tall hat and gloves on the floor. He turned then to Sproat, who had gone up first in proprietary fashion, also in case he missed anything. Now, the minister's tall form blocked retreat. For the first time, Sproat felt unease.

'You are a vile and mean lecher and blackmailer, and for that you must die and go to judgment.'

The stern voice overcame the great clock's unaltered ticking. Never had the Reverend Aeneas McPhail held an audience more intent than now. Sproat hit out, and the minister parried the blow. He lifted Sproat then in his powerful arms and carried him to the edge of the balcony. Sproat had begun to scream, and although there was nobody about McPhail covered the man's mouth meantime with a corner of his black coat, conquering his struggles. The clock began to whirr, ready to strike. McPhail's mind, in contemplation of murder, remained cool. Justice was about to be done, no more than that. He waited, mastering the other's struggles still, the coat's thickness keeping Bailie Sproat silent.

The clock chimed. In course of the great booming echo, McPhail cast Sproat over the balcony, limbs flailing, his cry of terror unheard in the remaining echoes of the chime. He hit the floor, and lay there writhing, not yet dead, his mouth a black open gasping shape.

'McPhail . . . McPhail . . .'

The sounds he made were deadened by the resumed ticking of the clock. There would be another chime shortly. McPhail raced downstairs.

'We will try again, bailie,' he said. 'Make no haste to die.'

He laughed, and picked up the broken shape that had once been a man; twitching, piddling, whimpering from its mouth, whence blood gouted already in a thin trickle. The fractured bones had no resistance and McPhail had no pity. This was the way of his ancestors, the outlawed clan whose name dared not be spoken by day; who would lay a hand in the dark on the shoulder of a friend, but would show no mercy to a foe. Upstairs again, carrying his mewling burden, the minister hastened, anxious not to miss the last chime. It was four o'clock.

'If you do not die this time, bailie, I will come down again and break your neck with my two hands after all,' he murmured. Again he cast Sproat with force over the side. The rag doll the man had become went down like lumber, and when the final chime sounded it was, this time, a bailie's wake.

The minister retrieved his tall hat and gloves from the floor and went downstairs for the last descent, taking one brief look at the body sprawled on the floor. Sproat was as dead as mutton. He himself could say with truth that he had come on business and found the bailie lifeless at the foot of the clock-tower. That the latter had had financial worries concerning cotton everyone knew; he had maybe not withdrawn his investments in time.

McPhail wiped the traces of blood and urine from his black coat with his handkerchief, put his hat on his head and went to tell the old woman at the lodge by the gate. She had seen him arrive alone.

* * *

The city was shocked at news of the death of so respected a figure as the bailie, and it was the more to be regretted as within weeks, word came of a bumper crop of cotton available in Deccan. The dead man had evidently had shares in that and in the rolling-stock needed for conveyance; if only he had held out for a week or two longer, he would have been as rich as Sir Phelim Orde in his day. The fleeting nature of human life was dwelt on at length by the Moderator himself in Glasgow Cathedral, the funeral being well turned out despite the rumour of suicide; in England that was notifiable, up here merely to be regretted. The Lord Provost and the bailies filed in with their chains of office and their cocked hats, the Moderator was entertained suitably afterwards, and everyone went home. It was noted that Mr McPhail had not offered to take part in the ceremony; no doubt he was still in too great a state of distress at the finding of poor Sproat's body. Multiple incarcerations, it was said, there had been; a shocking sight, no doubt.

A less charitable interpretation of McPhail's lack of appearance was that everybody knew Oakdale parish was going rapidly downhill, not only because of the late Sir Phelim Orde's bankruptcy but because of the minister's rumoured loose life. It was best not to show one's face in public more than could be helped in these circumstances, though of course McPhail still mounted his pulpit twice on Sundays for as many as still chose to attend.

* * *

Nancy had found the bloodstained handkerchief. She always cleaned out the minister's pockets, because like all men he filled them with everything under the sun and then forgot to empty them. At first she thought he'd had a nose-bleed, then realised what it was. She took the thing down to the fire which was kept stoked below the boiler in the kitchen, and stabbed at it determinedly with the poker among the hot coals till there was nothing left. Then she went, still flushed with the heat, to look at the coat again, with a fresh damp cloth in her hand. By the time she'd finished there was again nothing left to show outside or in the pocket, unless anyone looked the way the police could. As it was, nobody had thought of sending for them. She herself kept quiet. She wouldn't even tell the minister she knew.

She went then and found a freshly ironed handkerchief, and put it where the other had been. He'd never know the difference, having a mind on other things.

Neartmhor, by Inverness, 4th May

Dear Mr McPhail
I have to tell you that my niece Amy died yesterday, happy at last. We use the euphemism 'passed away', and this in fact is what happened almost visibly, as if she passed out of her body before our eyes to somewhere else. I am having her buried privately here; you are not expected to

attend the funeral.

However, I have a proposition to make. I myself will not live long, although at this moment I enjoy excellent health. My anxiety is for my beloved little Eddie now his mother is dead. He is not old enough to do without a guardian, as you will understand.

Although you and my niece did not see eye to eye in many things, she had a respect for you and often spoke of you. It occurred to me to wonder if you would, for a consideration of an allowance, undertake this kindness for the boy. As you are of an active cast of mind and body you will undoubtedly not want to allow either to vegetate, and the little parish a few miles off is in need of a minister. The duties would not be very arduous, and you would be interested in my library here, which has several hundred volumes concerning other faiths. To widen the mind is always beneficial, even here, as I have found personally.

All this will take you a little time to arrange if you will agree to it. Will you inform me at your convenience if this suggestion meets with your assent?

I remain, sir, your devoted servant,

Julius Towne

Uncle Julius, who had successfully shaken the pagoda tree long ago largely by persuasiveness, had too much natural tact to make clear in the above letter that he was already informed by way of Amy's mother, who had written lately with her new address, that the disgraceful state of affairs in Oakdale ought certainly to mean that the erring minister should be deprived of his incumbency as soon as possible. Unfortunately there was nothing in the bye-laws which allowed for this contingency unless the minister himself chose to resign.

The whole business had entertained old Julius notably, as the reason for Louisa's spite was plain; she herself had been asked to leave. He could never have endured living with her and had a respect for poor Amy's husband, who had done so for a long time now. It was true enough that the neighbouring parish needed a minister, and the gossip would not follow McPhail up here. Ahur, consulted, said the signs were favourable. Julius smiled, and added a codicil to his will; the guru might despise money, but he could give a little to his poor of Madras or, if he preferred, invest it in Deccan cotton. There had been a story in the Bible, which Julius still at times consulted, about the good and faithful servant who had multiplied his master's means. There would still be more than enough left over to launch Eddie on his chosen career as a sodger, also for him to enjoy life.

*   *   *

It was almost a year later, everything having taken a little time to arrange; there had been the necessary decorum shown over the whole transaction. By now, a new minister was installed at Oakdale, and a covered carriage was making its way slowly up into the Grampians, with certain persons inside. The reins were held by McPhail himself, grief having turned his hair less black than formerly, though still thick and imposing in what was now a ferrous grandeur. In fact he resembled an Old Testament patriarch about to leave his father's house and taking his flocks and herds with him, making a new life in the wilderness.

One member of the flock sat beside him, a small dark-haired girl. Her identity, if she had remained at Oakdale longer, would have been guessed at by her growing resemblance to her mother. In plain words, Phoebe was becoming plump. Her belongings, with the rest, were piled into the back, which was why they had not, all of them, made part of the journey by rail. The baggage included a harp, which McPhail had purchased from the final auditors after the decision that Crosslyon itself should be pulled down. Nobody could think what to do with so enormous a house in straitened times, and it was feared more folk might fling themselves from the clock-tower if it remained empty, as at present.

All that was left behind, if unforgotten. In the back, as well as the luggage and McPhail's necessary books, were three more travellers. One was increasingly seen to be Holy Joe Sproat's child and no other, and her appearance was one strong reason why McPhail had deemed it prudent to change her establishment to far parts. The child's official father was the late Sir Phelim Orde, and the nearest name McPhail could find to stress this fiction was Ophelia. There was no doubt that Ophelia was plain, with her straggle of fair hair and narrow features. She might improve. He strove to remember that she was after all Brabazon's flesh; but meanwhile could tell himself only that her birth had killed her mother. Perhaps this was the punishment of Divine Providence upon him for having cast Joe Sproat down to death. Nevertheless he would do the same again; and even now, with the child for the time unseen behind him, recalled how she was by no means the outcome of his own richly flowing seed, but of a leaked and straying sperm from a blackmailer's condom. The ways of the Lord were strange, but must not be questioned or ignored. He would do his best for Brabazon's girl, but in the nature of things could never send her south to be finished at Mrs McIntyre's; gossip would raise its head again even by then. If only Ophelia had Brabazon's blue eyes to comfort him! There it was, however: and she hadn't. Holy Joe would have been the first to applaud his own prudence in taking her well out of the way.

There were two more occupants in the back. Nancy, in a black bonnet with a ribbon as became her new station, wore a gold ring on her fourth left finger. Mr McPhail had said they'd best make it regular for the new parish. She didn't mind. She sat by herself, contentedly suckling a dark-haired baby boy, who had been born just before they left. He was the image of the minister.